The Innocent and Others

Stories

Jerry Whitus

For
Ann

These stories were previously published by the following literary journals:

"Restitution" in *Ploughshares*
"A House in the Woods" in *Tupelo Quarterly*
"Edith's Goats" in *The Carolina Quarterly*
"Danny's Pool" in *Chicago Quarterly Review*
"Turkeys" in *Concho River Review*
"We Recruits in Granny Pearl's Army" in *Jabberwock Review*
"Brothers-in-Law" in *Potomac Review* (The Cabinet, 2012-2013)

Contents

Restitution

Monte set his glass down and raised the gun, waved it around like a kid with a toy. Elgin sat across the table, his hands in his lap.

"Whatta you say I just shoot you right here and now?" Monte said, like he might or might not be kidding.

But then Elgin shot first, a sharp explosion, and Monte's eyes flew open, his shot went wild, his kneecap shattered. Elgin came up out of the chair—all five-foot, three inches of him—and, steadying the little Colt Vest Pocket model with two hands, let Monte have another bullet somewhere around the mouth. Finally, he yanked the trigger once again because he was scared and wanted to be sure.

Elgin looked around to see that the cafe was, indeed, empty. He was trembling, working hard to hold on to himself, aware of the scent of gunpowder and a sudden screaming silence. He got to the screen door, pushed it open, and paused for a moment on the porch, heaving to catch a breath of air and get his lungs working again. It was a mid-morning in June and sunlight put a sharp edge on roofs and store fronts across the way and on down the street. A dog was yapping, tearing up the thick, humid air. Elgin put the warm pistol into his jacket pocket. People were coming out of shops, stretching their necks to look his way. A few of them—Thom Simmons, Acy Stumph, the pharmacist's teenage son, Jay Archer, and one he didn't know—were in the street and started up toward the cafe to see what was going on.

Elgin left the porch and walked toward them, floating a little, a dandelion in the wind. When they met, Thom Simmons asked him, "What's happening up there?" And something else that didn't register. Elgin dropped his head, mute, and continued on down Travis to the next corner where the Hempel Furniture Store looked across the pavement at Betsy's Basket, a fabric and notions shop. He turned right there, feeling the eyes of the town on the back of his neck, and hurried in a frenzy on to where the pavement gave way to gravel and red clay and the Davis brothers had their auto repair garage in a wide-mouth metal building.

Outside, junk was stacked in neat, organized piles—a few old engine blocks, rusted muffles, tail pipes tied together and standing against the shaded wall, ruined tires one atop the other. Elgin passed out of the sharp sunlight into the coolness of the garage. "Where's Hardy at?" he heard himself say to Hardy Davis's big wife, who was standing just inside the entrance smoking, her hair tied into a knot on top of her head. She worked there answering the phone and keeping the books.

"Yeah," Hardy called from under a cream-colored Buick raised up on a pair of hydraulic jacks deep inside the building. The place was neat and swept clean—pegs for tools, shelves filled with parts in boxes, cans of motor oil and antifreeze, fan belts, and hoses hanging in their assigned places. Hardy kept it that way. He'd raise hell if you dropped a gum wrapper or cigarette butt or anything like that on his property.

Elgin noticed the way the light fell from a row of windows up near the roof line. A big fan on a pole in one corner was making a tiny racket. Elgin approached the Buick, kneeled down, and scrunched forward to look in under the car. It was cozy under there, Hardy's red face illuminated by a drop light. He was unscrewing the oil pan is what it looked like.

"Give me a minute," Hardy spoke again, like he could sense somebody watching him but wasn't troubled with who it was.

Elgin dropped onto his belly on the cool, gritty concrete. He spread his legs to get a purchase. He swallowed back something curdled that came up into his throat, then steadied the pistol with two hands to take aim. Hardy's ear got his attention. Elgin squinted, aiming at the earhole like you might aim at a bull's eye. The explosion reverberated, sending a shrill echo. The bullet traveled dead on through Hardy's earhole, spewing hardly any blood; it went on through and came out the other side, or so Elgin surmised. He squeezed the trigger a second time, *a tinny resonant blast*, but the third time, it clicked—empty.

His one good ear ringing, Elgin rose and dropped the pistol back into his jacket pocket. He went to the front of the Buick. Hardy's big wife stood at the entrance outlined by sunlight, glaring at him, a fist held up near her mouth. Elgin turned the handle lock on one jack and the front end of the Buick jerked, settling down at an angle with a *swish*. He started to release the other one but hesitated and didn't. All he had done was all he could bring himself to do. The job was finished. Elgin glanced back toward the sunlight. There was a hole left where Hardy's wife had been.

As he came out of the garage, squinting, Elgin saw a few men coming across the open field just beyond the dirt road. They paused and gathered into a bunch. They watched him. He watched them, his eyes burning. Layton Archer, the pharmacist, stepped out from the others and called out, breaking the silence.

"Elgin, what in thunder are you doin'?"

Elgin shuffled his feet, trying to think which way to run, but didn't say anything. Layton Archer motioned his boy to get back behind him with the others.

"You got a gun there, son?"

"I guess…yes sir," Elgin called back.

Acy Stumph and another man had begun circling around and, in a moment, started across the road some distance to Elgin's left.

"Is that Hardy Davis in there?" came from Layton Archer.

Elgin attempted to contemplate what would happen next, his knees jumping up and down, sun sparks bursting before his eyes. He glanced one way and another and, in a sudden fury, broke out running, head down, pedaling as fast as his short legs would pedal. He was aware of the pistol bouncing around in his jacket pocket and the sound of his feet hitting the packed earth and then hard pavement. At the corner of Travis Avenue, he glanced back and saw the men heading into the garage. He wheezed to catch his breath, grabbed at his pounding chest, and started trotting, fast walking, and running, in turn, up Travis. At the cafe, there were three or four on the porch, including Hattie Shultz in her cooking apron. They stood close together, watching him pass by. He trotted on to the Magnolia filling station where he left his pick-up, pumped the gas pedal twice, choked her, and, as he knew she would, the truck coughed and started.

He drove straight out of town, east past the last few houses into the sunlight. After a few minutes, he hung his head out the window so the breeze would dry the sweat and help clear his brain. Glimpsing the undulating flow of familiar landscape, he saw early summer crops and milk cows and a stretch of pine forest. The road dipped into a hollow shaded by big hardwoods, and he crossed Coushatta Creek. In another mile or so, he slowed and made a sharp left turn onto Henk Road.

Trudy Davis sat on her front porch steps in a housedress and sandals, her eyes pinched in thought, a claw hammer and an old Gold Metal flour sack in her lap. Her phone had already rung twice. The first time, it was her sister, broken up, blabbering foolishness until Trudy could coax the news out of her, and then finally saying she was going to get Mama and come straight out there. A moment later, it was her sister's preacher, assuring her he would be coming as well. As she hung up, barely grasping the truth, floating out of herself, Trudy's mind was called back to earth by the sudden notion that Elgin Wilkins might be on his way, too. Yesterday evening, the Caldwell boy had arrived at the house on his bicycle with a note from Elgin, the words scribbled on lined paper. *I want restitution*, it said, and made some demands—money, apologies. It seemed Elgin was in a fit over the catfish. Monte got a big kick out of it. "Restitution? Where'en fuck did Elgin Wilkins get a four-dollar word like that," he said to his brother over the telephone. "And says he's coming out here to get the damn fish head. You believe that?" Monte had sent a message back by the boy about meeting in town the next morning.

Elgin's stated fury was, in a way, a phenomenon. Ever since Trudy had known him, since grade school really, she had never seen Elgin make a fuss about anything, though he had been the butt of pranks and jokes, she guessed, all his life. Monte and Hardy were among those who liked to pick on him. True, Monte had a rabid streak that could turn nasty, but then poor Elgin was such a ready target. Born premature (it was said his mother had died of it), parts of him had never caught up with his age. He had an outsized head that now, at the age of twenty-two or so, sprouted wispy threads of yellow hair. He weighed maybe a hundred and thirty bony pounds. He had a complexion that wavered between pasty and dull pink, depending on the angle of the sun. And there was his left ear, which resembled a dried-up walnut husk and was useless as far as hearing was concerned. A lot of boys, and girls, too—not to mention some of the teachers (he was the slow one in class)—got a kick out of vexing and teasing Elgin Wilkins from time to time.

Trudy pressed a wadded kerchief to her nose, which had turned red and runny; she sniffled and blew. The skin beneath her eyes was puffed, her mind a cold flame, waiting for deep grief or anger or some such emotion to begin tormenting her. She was confused, ashamed of herself, as well, that finding tears for the terrible thing her sister had told her was so difficult at the moment. In fact, she was aware of feelings that wanted to fly in the opposite direction. True remorse was slow in coming because of shock or the fact she could hardly believe it all; this is the way her mind dealt with it just now.

She had started to worry the minute Monte strapped on his pistol that morning—not for him, but that he might get riled up and make a mistake and hurt poor Elgin when she knew all he had in mind was to play a game, maybe taunt and bully him a little. Monte liked to wear the pistol around town, had a State of Texas permit he was proud of. He and some friends formed a club where they practiced quick draw and shooting beer bottles out of the air and other cowboy tricks. Playing dress up, Trudy and the other wives called it, smiling and shaking their heads at one another.

Henk Road started out black tar, which soon became packed red dirt, dusty now since the spring rains had passed them by. Elgin drove slowly, shifting between first and second, careful to anticipate random washouts and stay in the ruts. He had forgotten to remove the denim jacket; cold beads of sweat trickled from his sparse hairline. On one side of the road, he passed Beau Wenchel's corn standing bright green and head high. On the other, there was a field of peas showing pale purple and white flowers to the horizon. His heart was a stone rattling his ribs. He squeezed his eyes shut to clear the glaze out of them; a sudden cold tear ran down his face. Relief, fear, regret—he wasn't sure, the magnitude of the morning beginning to overtake him. *God Jesus help.*

His daddy, a man of peace and strong opinions, would not be happy. He would have found another way to deal with this. But then his daddy wasn't fit to deal with much anymore. He was in a state home down near Beaumont on his back in a rough, cramped room with two other old men, a disheartening place that smelled of bedpans, Mentholatum, and idleness. He had gotten sick with emphysema (roll-your-own tobacco since the age of twelve) and, later, bouts of pneumonia, all complicated by an absence of mind much of the time. Seeing him frail like that was painful, a man who had always taken good care of his appearance. He took sponge baths in the tub, shaved in the evening before supper, and kept the ironing board close at hand.

Making the drive down there two or three times a week, Elgin would nearly always bring up the catfish—how he expected to see her that evening or how he had fed her some chicken livers or fresh maize or something else special, or how she had let him scratch her head again (even if she hadn't), or something else cheerful. He and his daddy had caught that big blue catfish, sixty pounds if she weighed an ounce, on a jug line they kept set and baited at the mouth of a deep inlet on the Neches River, which ran for a hundred and eight yards along the west boundary of their property, land his mother's daddy had purchased and settled.

They caught the catfish a year ago, about the time the old man began to rasp and wheeze and lose sleep over gummed up lungs. They pulled her out, slick and fighting, and carried her, the two of them, in a wet tarp to a spring fed stock pond in the pasture behind their house. His daddy, who knew all there was to know about catfish and the river and the thickets, as well, declared her a female. They started feeding her—minnows and chum (concocted mostly of whatever the river gave up) and cottonseed cake, sometimes stirring in slop that they prepared for a hog they were fattening up. The plan was to invite relatives and neighbors for a feast one day, but that day never came. They got attached to the fish like you might to any wild creature that is child-like and sagacious.

For fun, they worked at training her to feed inside a ring his daddy had fashioned from a willow branch and floated on the water. To experiment, Elgin started wading into the pond to place the food inside the ring; he would stand in the murky water and watch while the shimmering fish eased up to it and fed. After a few weeks, she got so trusting of his presence that she would nibble this and that out of his hand. Her countenance breaking the surface was that of an old wizard: sleepy eyes set way back, dangling whiskers sprouting five inches long from her chin. It got to where the minute Elgin put a toe in the water, she would come running.

Catfish don't hear with ears but sense vibrations. So, the next thing was to slip up to the pond quietly and beat a pie pan with a spoon. In sight of a second, that huge tail stirred the water and she would shoot like a torpedo for the ring. They had weeks of fun together, Elgin, his daddy, and the catfish, too.

The downside was that other creatures in the pond soon began to disappear—frogs, minnows, brim, crawfish. "We should've known she wasn't any pond fish," Elgin's daddy said early on. He said they either eat her as God intended or take her back to the river so she could live out her days. Elgin argued for the river and his daddy went along with it. First, they took the willow ring and placed it in a shaded spot under spreading limbs in an inlet of the Neches not far from where they had caught her. They filled the ring with chicken blood and chopped liver and cottonseed, which she was partial to. Then, they hauled her from the pond, carried her to the river, and slid her in. She sank, disappeared. "You can bet that was a surprise," Elgin's daddy said. At intervals, Elgin beat the pan with a rhythm: *ratta-tat, ratta-tat-tat…*over and over. Ten minutes went by, more. Gone, they figured, and then, timidly, her big mouth emerged inside the ring, just like before, to get her dinner. Elgin's daddy hooked an arm around his son's neck and squeezed and scrubbed his noggin. They hopped around, slapping one another and laughing like they hadn't done for a long time.

Elgin began feeding her every evening. Just after supper, he would make the walk down to the water, toss chum or whatever into the ring, beat the pan, and here she would come. Sometimes he'd strip down to his underwear (knowing better than to go into a muddy river with his privates exposed) and, hanging from a low branch, slip into the water with her. If anything, she seemed to welcome him. After a while, some neighbors and people from town showed up to marvel. A river biologist from the university Extension Service came one evening to investigate and wrote a story about it in their monthly newsletter.

From time to time, of course, she would venture out, be gone for a few days, but Elgin kept going down to the river early mornings and again about sundown, play the pan, and she would finally come up, fighting off others when necessary to get what was hers. Each reunion was a new thrill. In town, at the cafe or wherever, people would ask, "Where's that old blue cat?" or "Has she showed up yet?" teasing him as usual but with a certain respect, even a little local pride for what Albert Wilkins and his son had accomplished.

Now, on the narrow road, Elgin encountered a new Ford pickup and then a tractor trailering a load of hay, but he eased over to the side and neither paid him any attention. He stopped where a tiny steam trickled across the road. It was shaded by two cottonwoods and, in the distance, beyond the pale green of soggy pasture was a crop of sugar cane. Dried up with thirst, he got out of the truck and crouched down to drink, cupping the water, warm and grainy, but wet at least. He spit. He sat back in the sand, breathing pure, free air, thinking he hadn't thought enough about what all this was going to lead to, this deep hurt and anger. "Just stay away from them," his daddy had scolded when Elgin would complain about the teasing and bullying that came from the Davis brothers and others back in school a long time ago. "All that Davis bunch is arrogant and that's the worst sort of dumb," his daddy said. But, of course, he didn't understand how the remarks, the arm twisting and ear thumps and sharp jokes, isolated him, bent his spirit, and created the darkest of thoughts in his mind.

Trudy poured a glass of tea, went out, and settled on the porch steps again, wondering if she was crazy to think that Elgin might show up—or to be sitting there exposed if he did. She was wary, somewhat in doubt, but not really scared. *Whatever else, Elgin Wilkins is not any kind of monster*, her heart told her, and for a moment, an odd sense of freedom enveloped her and the house, as well. Relief was clear without saying it to herself. Her fat yellow cat rubbed up against her two or three times, searching for attention, and then sauntered over and gazed up at the catfish head as he had been doing since yesterday. It was nailed high up on the corner porch post, gnats buzzing around it now. The cat had worked himself silly trying to climb the post but had finally given up.

Trudy heard a vehicle. It wasn't a tractor. Her chest caved in. She breathed, nearly starting to count, like waiting for thunder after lightning. In a minute, the nose of Elgin Wilkins' half-ruined pickup appeared beyond her Ligustrum bush. He stopped in front, cut the engine. He glanced at her, then straight ahead down the road, so deep in the seat of the small, black truck he could barely see over the steering wheel.

Finally, Elgin climbed out. He took off his jacket, tossed it back into the cab and gently slammed the door. To his eyes, Trudy Davis seemed fresh as spring clover, sitting in the shade of the porch, holding a glass of tea in two hands. Still, as he advanced slowly up the yard path toward her, he couldn't help glancing up at the porch post, at the head of his catfish hanging there, her wide-set eyes disturbed, leathery mouth gapped open.

Trudy straightened and put on a face, pulling her hair back with one hand. "You don't have to tell me anything," she blurted at him. "People have been calling, driving me crazy."

Elgin felt his tongue curl but couldn't find a word to place there.

"My god, Elgin. Did you do what they told me? What's got into you?" She wanted to cuss, display murderous fury and hot tears, but Elgin appeared as meek as a dwarf in a fairy tale, recoiling a little with every word she spit at him. And having known him most all her life, the history of his life, she found it hard to hate with the hate that was her right and duty.

"Listen, I don't…" Elgin muttered, trying to arrange some plausible words.

"Gol, aren't you a least bit sorry? You shot him, they said, Monte. And my only brother-in-law. Did you go crazy?" Her mouth tightened and she rose a little. "Elgin, you're not going to hurt me, are you?"

"I never…. No," he said. "No, I wouldn't."

Trudy sighed and sniffled. She set the tea glass aside and held out the claw hammer. "Here, anyway, here—take the damn catfish," she said. Her eyes were squinting in fury, her sharp nose aiming at him.

Elgin took care working the nails loose, one and then the other, standing on a slat-bottom chair that Trudy had brought out from the kitchen. He swatted at gnats and two bottle flies that flew out of the hollow mouth. Naturally, the head emitted a ripe odor, but in Elgin's mind, the scent was no more than the Neches during a dry spell when the water went chocolate brown and still as the sky. He discerned no damage to the head, but then there wouldn't necessarily be any. Monte Davis and his brother hadn't used a hook or anything legal—but electric wires to stun the fish and get her out of the water. They had floated down river early in the morning and dropped wires in the inlet was the way it was told to Elgin. Monte had come into town bragging about it, saying that they were going to have a fish fry. He and his brother had caught a blue catfish big enough to feed half the community, and they could thank Elgin Wilkins for it. It wasn't a stretch to know what he meant. He invited everybody to drive by his place and look at the head on the porch post, nine inches between the eyes, he claimed.

After hearing of Monte's rampage, Elgin went down to the river. There was still a scattering of fish floating belly up in the inlet like flotsam, a bunch of red ear bream washed against the bank. Elgin choked, bent over gasping, and then an anger rose out of the river, crept up his bare feet, through his body, consuming his brain. He went to the house, took his daddy's little pistol from the pine cabinet where they kept their shotguns, and started practicing with it, aiming at yellow plums in a tree they had planted in the orchard.

Elgin tossed the hammer into the grass in front of the porch and slid the head of his catfish into the flour sack Trudy had provided. She came back from a phone call and held out a glass of tea.

"Drink it down, hear. That was my sister again. They're on their way right now." She breathed a breath that made her flat chest expand. "Elgin, you are in so much trouble, a mess that is going to haunt you, and you are going to suffer. I hope you appreciate that."

Trudy McNeece—that was her name back then—wasn't the fairest girl in school, due partly to how her teeth and gums stood out whenever she smiled. But she was always clean and trim in fresh dresses and sometimes ruffles, her pale orange hair pinned nicely. She was liked all around and she had always been kind to him. At one time, in a dream maybe, he had believed that she was even fond of him. That's where Elgin's mind settled for moment, there on a memory of her young face. He drained the tea glass. A calmness washed over him, but then in the next minute, a bitter knot appeared in his throat. He wanted to say sorry for the harm and outcome of it all but, exposed in front of her, couldn't utter the word forgive.

Then, as he was leaving, walking the path out to his truck, toting the bulging flour sack, he felt a presence come up behind him. The air grew warm and the clean laundered scent of her settled into the space around him. Yet, when he turned back, she was still on the porch steps. He gazed at her feet, her naked ankles through the sandals, tiny yellow flowers decorating her cotton dress.

"Elgin, you know they are going to catch you," she said. "You have got nowhere to go except out in the thickets, the swamp, and nothing good is going a come of that. They'll come with dogs and you know what that means. You got no hope, except I believe some of those in town will speak up for you…if you give yourself up. I have always known you were liked, and they respected your father. Elgin, you might as well sit down here on the steps with me and wait for them."

Trudy scooted over, making room, a sort of smile on her face. It was all Elgin could do not to do what she wanted him to. The possibility of it stood in front of him.

I can't, his mind said. "I can't," he said out loud to Trudy Davis, just shy of trusting her.

He backed up a step, turned, and crossed the yard to the road, carrying the flour sack. He put on his jacket. He climbed into the truck, cranked the engine, and felt for the empty pistol in his pocket. Then, he headed out in the direction he was pointed, away from town.

A House in the Woods

His name was Rodrick and they called him Roddy. He was fourteen, a little short for his age, restless by nature, smart enough and, due to his parents, mostly tried to do the right thing. When this began, this unlikely dark journey, it was the middle of February, a raw, freezing afternoon, threatening sleet and rain. The boy had borrowed his father's deer rifle, which was allowed now, and gone into the woods to hunt for feral hogs that had invaded the community and his father's property as well, first tearing up the cow pasture and then a corner of the orchard and then escaping into the woods to do their damage there.

Wild hogs were what everybody, meaning the boys at school, were talking about. And then the town officials put a bounty on them, six dollars for every tail brought in. That and, even more, the pride that would come with it had set Roddy's imagination on fire.

At his father's insistence, they spent a morning sighting the rifle and shooting cans and bottles off a stump. Once satisfied, his father scrubbed the top of his son's head. "Before you shoot, look for a tree to climb in case you miss," he said, smiling a little.

It was a few days later that Roddy got into the woods. The sky was low and dark gray above the trees, most of them stripped bare so a person could imagine they might never recover. Needles of ice had formed along the banks of a creek that seldom dealt with ice even in the middle of winter. Wearing a dark wool coat, a cap his mother had knitted, high-topped canvas sneakers, and carrying the rifle, Roddy came down out of the woods over a fallen tree into the creek bottom. By now, his cheeks were chapped raw and his big ears nearly purple due to the cold wind.

All afternoon he had seen nothing stirring, not a squirrel or rabbit or even a bird, but there were fresh signs of wild hogs—the fallen leaves and black earth torn up in patches to get at roots a foot deep.

Roddy stopped at the edge of the creek, took a sandwich from his coat pocket, and lifted the white bread to inspect the jam—fig. He chewed, gazing down stream to where it turned under the branches of withered trees. By this time, he had grown anxious, anxious with the silence and anxious for something to shoot at.

Now he kneeled, cupped his hands, and drank from the creek, shivering. With frozen fingers, he lifted the rifle and started downstream. Across the creek were high banks and, on top of them, dull green patches of gallberry and dried up cane. He went on to where the creek turned, found a rippling shallow spot, and crossed over, soaking his shoes. He climbed the bank. Beyond it was a field covered with bush and brambles and beyond them the start of a pine forest. It was there beneath the trees that he saw a moving shadow, or thought he saw one. In a rush, he started toward it, walking fast and then nearly running. He slipped off the trigger safety, reached a clump of berry vines, and stopped there beside them, trying to locate among the trees what he was nearly sure he had seen. There was nothing, not until he glanced to his left into the heap of briars and saw not a hog or any kind of animal, but a figure that seemed to resemble some part of a man. A man stretched out in there among the web of vines, nearly hidden.

Quickly, Roddy stepped back, looked around and then up at the sky, taking in a breath of air to clear his mind. He looked again and, sure enough, it was what his eyes had already told him. He retreated a few steps and steadied himself to get a better look. Gripping the rifle, he waited, watching, but the figure was stone still. "Mister," he finally heard himself utter. "Mister!" he called out, then eased closer. It was a big man laying on his side, his legs drawn up a bit. He wore muddy rubber boots, a canvas coat with red patches on the elbow, and a hat with earflaps that

Roddy could just make out through the briars. Nearby, beyond the briars, as if tossed aside, was a cloth shoulder bag and a small garden spade.

Run, Roddy's mind and legs tried to tell him, and he wanted to run, felt it in his whole body, but couldn't get started. At the very least, the man was in trouble. The boy moved closer, observing how the man was tangled deep in the briars. He laid the rifle aside, dropped to his knees, and gripped one of the rubber boots. He shook it back and forth, carefully at first, and then more violently. "Are you sleeping! Asleep! Are you asleep!" Roddy exclaimed and yelled and then listened to the silence. He stood up and walked a circle, his knees jumping. He looked down at his hands, showing points of blood where the thorns had bit him, and he was scared.

Nonetheless, he went back, grasped the man's boot with both hands this time, gritted his teeth, and yanked. Yanked and pulled, yanked and pulled, managing at last to get enough of him out of the briars to take a shoulder and shove him over. It was an old man he was looking at, but not just any old man, a man he knew, a man they called Mr. McHenry.

Roddy backed up, knelt down in the weeds, and placed the rifle at easy reach, light-headed, nearly sick in his stomach. Never had he seen a dead man who was not dressed in a dark suit and tie, carefully groomed, lying in a coffin. This man's face was lined, full of veins and indentions, bristled whiskers that could have been on a nettle. One damp eye was open just a little, and on his caved-in cheeks and forehead were small dots of dried blood like those on his own hands.

This Mr. McHenry was well known in town. You would see him idling on one of the benches in front of the merchant store with his wife, a stout, pink-cheeked old woman who fixed her white hair in a braid around her head and wore a long dress with a collar, the same dress all the time it seemed.

Roddy pictured them bent over a gadget the old man used to crack pecans. He would set a pecan upright under a plunger and push it down so the shell cracked like there were seams in it. He would peel the hull away, pick the meat out with a thin blade, and pass the perfect halves to his wife, who filled small paper sacks you could buy for a quarter. People stopped and talked with them. They laughed. They bought the oily sacks of pecans and passed them to the children.

As the picture lingered, Roddy's eyes began to cloud up. He rubbed his face with both hands and gazed down at them, red and chapped.

The walls of the world he knew seemed about to cave in. He looked at the winter sky above the pine trees and, for the first time, thought of his father. It was nearly evening and would soon be dark. His mother would be in the kitchen by now, but this time of year his father, who worked for the county, was never home until well after night had set in.

Roddy had no clear idea what he ought to do. *Head home for help,* his mind told him, and then he thought, *stay with the old man.* His father would come, shooting into the air to get his attention. He considered one thing one moment and then the opposite. He stood up and gazed at the old man again. He seemed calm, comfortable, like he had just decided to lie down in those unwelcoming briars and go to sleep. At the same time, Roddy felt overwhelmed and without prospects, and then came a renewed urge to start out toward home. He retrieved the rifle and right away remembered the wild hogs, how they rampaged and tore up the earth, what they could do to a body.

There beside the old man's shoulder bag was the spade. He opened the flap of the bag and found a muddy hatchet, a long butcher knife, and beneath them, a pile of hairy roots half-covered with mud. An old man out alone in this cold digging roots.

Restless, he took the hatchet and the spade and went down to the bank overlooking the creek, moved into the cane, and started digging, chopping. The ground was hard, but he had strong shoulders and a renewed determination. He took an armload of cane back up to the old man and spread it over him. Three armloads he cut and carried and piled up, which pretty much did the job. He returned for one more load. A mound of cane was the old man's grave for now, Roddy telling himself it was some kind of protection, almost believing it.

At last, he raised the rifle and shot towards the pine woods, three sharp explosions and then one more, something he had been itching to hear all afternoon. The kicks against his shoulder were a comfort, the hope it would scare away any animal out there more comforting still.

It was just about dark now, but there was not a star or friendly light. He made his way to the bank and slid down on his butt, crossed the creek through freezing water, went up the far side, and continued on into the woods, which offered a sudden darkness he hadn't expected, the deep darkness of winter. The trunks of trees were pitch black; after a few steps, he couldn't see his feet. He started out through low branches and thick vines he didn't see until they were on him. He considered turning back to follow the creek, which would be easier but a longer walk than going through the woods to his house. Without making a conscious decision, he went on, sure that if he kept a straight line, he would end up at a neighbor's fallow cornfield where he'd be able to see the lights of his own house.

"Hell fire," he said to hear the sound of his own voice. "Hell fire," he said louder to warn ghosts and devils that kept trying to float out of the trees into his head. Using the rifle barrel to clear the way, he would start through a patch of thick or thorny bush and then search right and left to find a way around them, all the while disturbed by the rustle of dead leaves under his feet.

Suddenly, he heard a long, drawn-out sound that seemed to be traveling through the treetops, a kind of pathetic moaning. He pointed the rifle, shivering a little, and soon recognized the hoots and shrieks of an owl, the only living sound he'd encountered all afternoon. An owl searching the frozen night for something to eat was nothing to worry about. In a while, the canopy opened up a bit and there was a bit of light.

Stretching his legs, he came out of the trees into a clearing. The sky had changed. On the horizon were a few frail stars. He thought of his mother and sister, the warm light of the kitchen. They would be asking after him, peeved at first but then growing concerned. And he imagined his father, wondering if he could be home yet, and it came to him that he was totally ignorant of how far he had come or how much time had passed.

Hurrying then, he crossed the clearing and came to a growth of young pines probably planted by a timber company. He couldn't recollect ever seeing them. It scared him. His mind had been saying, *go straight ahead*. Now, which way was straight ahead?

With some effort, he pushed through the small, prickly pines, came out of them, and suddenly found himself stumbling down a steep slope into a gully, losing his rifle, finding it, and clambering up the other side.

He stood on the ridge, catching his breath, wondering how to go on. He was lost, dead tired, and had no idea which way to turn. Then, he heard the owl again—long, rising hoots and shrieks up ahead, as if they were traveling the same trail and doing it of the same mind. With rising confidence, Roddy followed his ears to a path of sorts that eventually widened and continued under the black limbs of big trees. Before long, he was circling a pond. The wind came up, rippling the black water.

There was more. The path descended through a shallow marsh; thin plates of ice crunched underfoot. Overhead were wisps of clouds and scattered stars, and it seemed the owl, who had been calling out to him from time to time, had decided to leave him. At the same time, Roddy's feet seemed to know the way to go. He came to a tumbled down rock wall, the kind people built a hundred years ago. Farther on was a fenced-in plot that seemed to have once been a garden or orchard, skeletons of ruined trees. It was all strange to him. He pushed through a hedgerow onto a dirt road, narrow and two-rutted. Up ahead was a small house with two lit windows. It looked settled, as if purposely set there, waiting to be found. There was a bottle tree out front and nearby a small shed. Roddy expected dogs, country people kept dogs. None came out for him.

He crossed under the porch roof, leaned the rifle against a stack of firewood out of sight, and knocked softly. When nothing happened, he knocked again, louder than he meant to. In a moment, the door cracked an inch. It swung open.

"Well?" a woman said, stepping back into a dim light.

Roddy lowered his head.

"What's that you're doing?" the woman said. "Come on closer, so I can see you." She squinted at him. "You a boy?"

"Yes, ma'am."

"What are you doing out there?"

"I got lost."

"Lost?" She stood eyeing him for a moment. "Lost boy. Well then, come in out of the dark," she said, and Roddy stepped inside, immediately grateful for the warmth, the pale light. It was a large room, a kitchen, but more than a kitchen. It smelled of cedar and something cooking. An iron stove stood in the middle of the room, flames dancing about in cracks around the door. A table with two lit kerosene lamps on top of it. Cane chairs. Long shadows lay across the floor.

"Your feet's wet," the woman said to him.

"Yes, ma'am."

"You better take'em off before they're froze stiff."

She was a small woman, shorter than him and quite old. She wore a long dress with a bib apron over it. Hair white as combed cotton fell to her shoulders. Her face was pink and deeply creased in the lamplight. She had a nose with a hump on it. More than anything, it was the long hair that confused him, made him hesitate, unsure. But sitting before the stove, removing his shoes as she had ordered, he glanced up, searching her features until there was no doubt he knew who she was.

"Lay the socks there," she said, indicating the stove top. "And your cap too. What's your name?"

Roddy couldn't speak, nor breathe, nor work his mind either. He sniffled, wiped his nose, tried to swallow the knot in his throat.

"Shy. Boys your age are often shy. Or has the cat got your tongue?"

"You got a cat?"

She laughed. "That's a good one. You got me there."

She studied his face as if trying to figure him out. He glanced at a sink with a hand pump for water, a wood cook stove with pots on it. "You're about froze, I guess."

"Yes, ma'am."

"You look old enough for coffee," she said, at last. "You drink coffee?"

Roddy nodded his head, the most he could do just now.

"I was about to make some, so I'll fix yours with hot milk while you take off your coat and get your tongue back."

When she turned to draw water at the sink, Roddy stood and removed his coat, examining the room. There was a collection of calendars on one wall, some smoky old pictures in frames. In a far-off corner, a high iron bed and shelves led back into shadows. Farther back were sacks and things of different shapes and sizes, some hanging from rafters.

"Have I seen you before?" the woman said, again studying his face.

Roddy told her that he went to town sometimes with his mother and his sister.

"What's your name?"

He told her.

"Roddy, huh…" she uttered, as if she didn't much care for it.

She came from the cook stove, sat a glass on the table, and poured in an inch of thick black coffee, which swirled through steaming milk as she added it. "You'll like it sweet," she said, spooning in a ribbon of syrup from a fruit jar. Satisfied, she beat all that together until it might have been chocolate milk or muddy creek water.

She watched as he lifted the glass. "Good," Roddy said after a sip, the smooth, sweet drink warming his throat.

"Our kids were drinking milk coffee before your age." She sat down across from him with her own coffee steaming in a blue cup. "You probably didn't know it, but it's going to snow soon," she said, breaking a silence. "I can always tell from the minute I get up. I told Henry this morning he better get home early and now it's after dark. He used to be by the clock. Our supper's on the stove, though. We'll wait a little if you can stay."

When he didn't say anything, she went on. "He'll be happy to see a boy here. Corn soup's what we often have on nights like this, and bacon. Cornbread. No greens this time of year. What are you doing way out here, huntin'?"

"Yes, ma'am. I mean, no, ma'am."

She laughed. "Which is it?"

"Not huntin'. Walking." Holding the glass with two hands, Roddy sipped the hardy mixture. It was satisfying. "And I was chasing a hog," he added.

"A hog? Who would think that?"

Stupid thing to say. He blushed, not knowing why he had lied. "Anyway, I just got lost."

"Your mother'll be worried. I used to worry about my boys and the girl, too. Now there's just Henry to worry about. He knows better but goes out in the cold anyway and has no sense of time. By the time you drink that, he'll probably be here." A slight smile bunched the wrinkles in her cheeks. "And we can have supper and he'll walk you to the Bridgers down the road. It might be snowing by then, but the Bridgers own a telephone and car and they'll get you home. You don't need to worry."

At once, she coughed into a frilly handkerchief, settled herself, moved her cup aside, and told him she was going out for firewood. As she stood up, Roddy jumped to his feet. He remembered the rifle on the porch and didn't want to be caught in a lie. "I'll get the firewood," he said in a hurry. "I always get it at home."

Barefoot, bareheaded, he went out and closed the door tight behind him. There were no stars in sight, but the wind was up. And somehow the bottle tree, shown in its perfect solitude, faintly chimed. Listening, straining his eyes to peer as deep as possible into the night, he noticed a movement in the yard. As his eyes adjusted, he saw a dark figure rise up, hesitate, and come toward him, one ghostly image at first, then another and another. Three large hounds they were. They came on to the edge of the porch and looked at him down long noses, as if sizing him up, their eyes glinting in the faint window light. One of them, the largest, whined, whimpered, but there was no barking, no growling, no coming at him. Nonetheless, Roddy reached for the rifle and they sat back on their haunches the way experienced dogs would. He held the rifle loosely in his hands and then quickly put it back, gathered sticks of firewood, and made his way inside.

"Told me he was going to dig sassafras roots," the woman said, opening the door to the stove as soon as Roddy had come in. "He said he knew where some was and he's been promising me a bunch to cook with. People make tea, but I like to pound'em and boil'em in my cooking sometimes. That's what my mother did. And that's a long time ago."

She stoked the crimson bed of coals with a metal rod and told him to lay in a few sticks. Then, she slammed the iron door and latched it shut. With smoke dissipating in the air, Roddy eased into his chair, slipped on the warm, dry socks, slid his feet under the stove, and opened his mouth and told her about the dogs. "There's three big dogs out front," he said, his voice gaining strength. He described them hunched under the bottle tree.

"They're out there waiting for Henry," she told him. "As soon as we came to this place, they took up with him. He feeds them. But often they eat out of the woods. Follow him through the thickets or else come back here and wait for him just about every day. On nights like this, he fixes a pallet in the shed."

She rattled the pots on the stovetop, took down a skillet from an overhead hook, and, in a minute, he could smell bacon frying. Her movements were quick, vigorous, like his mother's when she was working over the stove. The bacon began to pop. She nodded toward the water pump over the sink and told him to take the bar soap and wash his hands. "Scrub'em good," she said, with a familiarity she hadn't used before. "Clean hands, clean heart," she told him.

A few minutes later, she came to the table with two bowls, heat rising out of them, along with spoon handles. "It's too hot to put in your mouth. We'll wait a minute," she said, and placed before him a square of cornbread and a thick strip of bacon on a small platter.

Instead of sitting, she went to one of the front windows, cupped her hands against the glass, and peered out. After a minute, she went to the other window and did the same. "Nope," she said, turning back.

I can wait if you want to, Roddy almost said. But then was glad he hadn't, hadn't told such a terrible lie. More lies had already spun in his head and out of his mouth than he could deal with. His stomach was churning now. He was scared, scared of her, of what he knew.

Miz McHenry went over and warmed her hands at the stove for a moment. She sat down and reached across the table. "Give me your hand," she said. He slid a hand toward her. She covered it with her warm, surprisingly soft one, dropped her head, and muttered a prayer, which he couldn't make out. She raised her eyes. A blue vein in her neck stood out. "Well," she said, "we'll go ahead then."

But as he started to eat, Roddy couldn't bring himself to lift the spoon. He was too drained, shaky, not because he was tired, but because he had done everything wrong. He wished he had been forthright and found the courage to take her hand and comfort her, that he hadn't left Mr. McHenry alone in the woods with all that could happen to him, that he hadn't believed he could handle anything when there were so many questions going in and out of his head.

What he did know is that he was going to have to find a way to tell her. Not right now, but soon. Why other than that was he here?

Coffee

The first deception is that it's a perfect spring day, generous sunlight, trailing clouds, a soft breeze, the sort of day William Wordsworth might call for in poems that appear in high school textbooks. Nonetheless, Lewis Means, a diligent man, is indoors at his usual coffee shop bent over a laptop crunching numbers and has been since early afternoon. He will take a corner table near the plate glass window, order a double expresso with a shot of water, and work for two hours or so nearly every afternoon. Today, the place is busy, full of chatter, customers coming and going.

After surveying the people nearby, Lewis downs the last drop of espresso and heads for the restroom to rinse his mouth. It's what he does after drinking coffee, due to his teeth. There is nothing to distinguish his looks, trimmed brown hair, an oval face, slightly pale complexion with a few tiny pits in his cheeks and rather narrow shoulders—except when it comes to his teeth. He is blessed with straight, bright, even teeth, to the point that women will sometimes comment on them or say something about his smile. Naturally, he doesn't want them stained, which is an ongoing problem since in an average day, he drinks several cups of coffee, rinsing after each one of them when he can. An obsession for sure, but one that, in his mind, is completely justified.

So, Lewis goes into the restroom, rinses his mouth, which takes twenty seconds or so, and immediately feels an urge to relieve himself, which sometimes happens after you run cool water over your hands. As he zips up, someone raps on the door, gently at first and then louder, loud enough to be rude. He flushes, washes up quickly, dries his hands, and opens the door to find a bunch of high school kids lined up at the counter. Pushing his way through the line, he goes back to his table, sits down to work, and right away begins to get an itchy feeling, a premonition that the world's not right, like when you're in the woods walking through high grass and hear something rattle. He looks around and, sure enough, his phone is nowhere to be seen, not under the notepad where he often hides it, not behind the screen of his laptop, or on the chair across the table or in his shoulder bag or on the floor. The phone is gone.

Flushed with disbelief, then an expanding anger, he sits back, folds his arms, searching the faces of the people around him. No one is sneaking glances his way, ducking, preparing to leave, or suspicious looking; everyone is occupied, playing with their phones or talking as usual, well behaved, decently dressed.

He studies the two girls behind the counter, busy with their disgustingly young customers and then, not to waste another second, closes the laptop and hurries outside into the sunshine. On the street, cars and pickups are coming and going, as they're supposed to. He gazes up the empty sidewalk and then in the opposite direction. A young couple carrying books is walking toward him and beyond them, halfway down the block, is a kid, striding along like he has somewhere important to go. Lewis starts after him, a black kid with a distinctive head of hair, short, thin, in a black T-shirt. Faster and faster, Lewis walks and then starts jogging. He yells, "Hey, just a minute. Hey!" waving a hand over head. The kid turns, sees him, backs up a step and takes off running, not down the sidewalk, but off the curb to cross the street. The first car to hit him is a big, white Buick, not straight on, but at an angle, knocking him onto the pavement out in front of a pickup going in the opposite direction. Braking tires squeal, a car smashes into the back of the truck. Lewis's head explodes.

Traffic stops and one by one people start getting out of their cars. A second later, phones come out. Lewis feels a shiver shoot through his limbs and then a desperate fear, like he's heard the snap of a major bone. Slowly, he moves to the curb, stands there, watching the turmoil, and then the excitement on individual faces. His conscience tells him to get out into the street and help, but his legs won't let him. A crowd forms around the kid, some people kneeling. Lewis stretches his neck, trying to see through them but can't. In fact, he can't get a clear fix on anything at all just then.

Slowly, he backs out of the sunlight under the awning of a smoke shop and stands there against the plate glass window trying to breathe. *If I had my phone*, he thought, *I'd call an ambulance.* But that's the whole problem, no phone. And before long, a new horror begins to swirl in his head. He has to get out there into the street and retrieve his phone, right then, otherwise he could have a lot of explaining to do. In a moment, a big bearded guy wearing a blue apron comes out of the smoke shop and, as the door closes, the sweet, rich scent of tobacco settles over the sidewalk, a brief distraction that is suddenly swept away by the screams and echoes of a siren, one and then more than one.

A patrol car arrives and then an ambulance. Two medics jump out, clear the crowd, and go to work. Watching all that action makes Lewis feel hopeful, but a brittle sort of hope that begins to break up piece by piece as he comes to realize that he has left his laptop back there on the table in the coffee shop, all those rowdy kids around it. And so, he's caught in a frantic dilemma, try to recover the phone and take a chance on losing his computer, which is filled with his clients' records, the intricacies of his job, his own financial secrets, or forget the phone and head for the coffee shop.

For a moment he hesitates—go, stay—until at last, taking a final look at the crowd of onlookers, the policeman, the medics, the wrecked truck with JB PLUMPING lettered on the door, he starts for the coffee shop, making his way through groups of people who have come out of the stores and offices onto the street and sidewalk. He pushes through the turmoil in front of the coffee shop and the moment the door closes behind him, one of the girls behind the counter, a girl named Janette with steaked red hair, holds up a cell phone.

"I think this is yours," she says. "Somebody found it in the bathroom."

∾

A few minutes later, Lewis leaves the coffee shop gripping his shoulder bag, takes one quick look down the street at the ambulance, its back doors flung open, waiting to be part of a scene he doesn't want to witness, hurries straight to his car, and drives home.

Well, not exactly home, but to his mother-in-law's house which rests in an old neighborhood of ancient shade trees and brick streets not far away. He and his wife came here to this small city, her hometown, in eastern Texas three weeks ago to make arrangements for her mother, who is already pretty far gone, to settle into a nursing home. Then, in a rush, his wife flew off to Tennessee to help her sister, who was suffering complications trying to have a baby, her third kid.

Lewis parks on the curved drive under a big pecan tree. Inside, smoky light from tall windows and musty scents and furnishings from another era. Nothing but ghosts to greet him, which makes him feel both relieved and like an intruder who has no business being here and might be caught at something. Then, as he heads down a dusky hallway to the bedroom, his wife calls. He glances at the screen and turns off the phone. He drops his shoulder bag on the bed, undresses, and, stark naked, goes back down the hall, takes a long shower, and then stands at the bedroom window drying off. There is a broad view of the backyard—plots of blooming flowers that need tending, persimmon and cedar elm trees, and a bank of azaleas that mark the boundary of the property. Lewis lingers in the muted light, dismayed once again at how the afternoon has betrayed him. Of course, there is nothing to help it; it's done, and chances are, he manages to tell himself, the kid, who is obviously healthy, even athletic, is going to be all right. In fact, any other outcome would make the smooth contours of his life a brutal deception, which doesn't make any sense at all.

He dresses, brushes his hair at the bathroom mirror with a little shaping cream to get the part right, and has a short, pleasant conversation with his wife, just the way she likes it, he likes it, and everything nearly normal. In the parlor, he has a tumbler of bourbon while watching the national news, has dinner from the refrigerator, and crosses the red brick street in front of the house and heads out for a walk through the neighborhood all the way to his wife's old elementary school, through the playgrounds and then around the perimeter of a city park.

Whenever the boy tries to appear, he manages to wave him away. Back home in the kitchen, he makes some strong coffee and sits down at the breakfast table with his laptop to go back to work, starting where he left off that afternoon.

He is a purchasing agent for an ambitious appliance manufacturer and has to keep up a steady pace or the work will bury him. Just about everything is done online and with spreadsheets. He haggles with suppliers, usually by email, places orders, fixes problems, and tracks shipments to wherever they are supposed to go in the U.S. or Canada or other places. It is a life of sitting still, working brain and fingers, pleasing bosses and everybody else on both ends of a deal, which suits him fine. Having the rules and regulations dictated seems to set him free, at least from making major decisions or exposing himself. When the old clock on the kitchen wall chimes eleven, he closes out, making his way around dark corners and down the hall to bed.

The first time he opens his eyes, it is 1:37 a.m., and except for the green numbers floating on the face of the clock, the bedroom is pitch-black. He lays waiting for his eyes to adjust and still it is black, so black that he isn't entirely sure he's awake. Don't start thinking about it, something in the air whispers and, immediately, he is thinking about it, about how the phone had magically disappeared and reappeared, how the kid had sauntered and then suddenly ran, how the car that hit him was white and the JB Plumbing truck was black, how improbable it would be for anyone to suspect or charge him with anything. He hadn't been seen chasing the kid into the street, hadn't pushed him, nor was he near enough to save him. Nevertheless, seeds of fear and guilt have taken root in his brain and he feels trapped, misused by fate. He considers going to the kitchen to pour a drink or make some coffee but instead, like one of those roly-poly bugs he liked to play with as a kid, curls into a tight ball and shuts his eyes.

He sleeps, he wakes, he sleeps again. At dawn, with pale orange sunlight creeping through the thick windowpanes into the bathroom, Lewis washes his face, goes to the kitchen, and makes coffee while eating a handful of grapes. He drinks one cup standing at the kitchen sink, rinses his mouth, pours another cup and sits down at the table, opens the laptop, and, in his undershirt and plaid pajama bottoms, gets back to work.

When the clock chimes eight, Lewis raises his head, jarred by the thought of the local paper, which he finds outside on the grass under a twisted, old dogwood tree. Sitting on the front steps, he tears off the dew damp plastic cover and there on the second page is a stark headline above a disappointingly short article with no pictures. "...a local boy, Ibram Betts, thirteen, was hit by a car or possibly a pickup truck on North Dixon in front of the county municipal offices...." is the essence of what it says. "...taken to the hospital by ambulance and then the ICU due to complications from a possible concussion and leg injuries...." Lewis runs his eyes back over the words he's just read, folds the thin paper, and pauses to let out a breath he doesn't realize he was holding. His heart rate speeds up. Deep in some merciful corner of his mind, he's relieved—a possible concussion and possible broken leg, what the hell, not so bad. It's over, he tells himself.

Making an effort to sound cheerful, he phones his wife, waking her. All's well, she tells him, her sister is doing fine, upstairs nursing the baby right then, although the kids are driving her nuts. "Next time we talk about getting pregnant, remind me of these two," she says. The truth is, his wife is overjoyed not to have to go to work. She has used the news about her mother to take a leave of absence from her job publishing catalogs for an outdoor clothing company, a break that has greatly improved their relationship. Depending on how long her mother hangs on, there could be a decent inheritance and money coming from the sale of the house.

Working alone in the kitchen, drinking his own coffee, Lewis can breathe again, his windpipe wide open, his heart beating in a nice, silent rhythm and his polluted conscience given over to a kind of recovery. After a while, however, he begins to feel restless from head to toe, and then a bit lonely, and finally impatient for a wider, clearer view of the world, which is unusual. He pulls on a pair of khakis and a Pittsburgh Pirates sweatshirt, drives to McDonald's to pick up a cup of coffee at the window, and starts driving out into the countryside. After a while, he turns off the highway onto a Farm to Market road that soon enters a pine forest. Big shaggy pines lit by sunlight and then hardwood trees loaded down with new leaves. He stops for a while on the banks of a shallow river, takes pictures of ducks and mud hens and big white birds with long yellow legs.

The road goes on through acres of meadows and plowed fields sprouting early crops. He stops in a little town for coffee and later has a late lunch and then gets lost at a crossroads that confuses the GPS tracker. Farther on, he has the unusual pleasure of asking for directions from a nearly toothless old man on a tractor and gets home at dusk.

He has made decisions. In the kitchen, he rinses his mouth, running his tongue back and forth over his teeth, then finds the phone number and calls the hospital, the only one in town. Playing a role, he asks the woman who answers to connect him with someone who can provide information about the boy and gives her his name. "Nope, we can't do that on the phone," she says. He tells her that he's a friend of the family. "Well, you'll have to ask the family then."

A little wired and confounded, Lewis considers how much of his busy life this god-awful thing is gobbling up and wants nothing more than to pack his bags and leave, like a modern-day wanderer passing through a cursed town. Instead, he pours bourbon with a little water into a heavy crystal cocktail glass that once belonged to his wife's father. He offers the old man, a lawyer he had never met, a belated toast, wondering what he would have to say about all this mess. Recovering the morning paper, he sits in the old man's small study in the shadow of law books shelved like a monument to order on two walls of the room. Then, skimming the article again, it seems as if a string of new words has somehow bled onto the page, words that are much more ominous than before...*concussion, damaged legs, ICU* are images that won't relent.

No, it's not over, his conscience tells him, not half over. Lewis stands, draws the heavy velvet curtains back, and looks out at the green departing day. *Go home*, he thinks, far away, north to familiar surroundings where it's safe to cross a street. It will be easy enough to phone and tell his wife that something urgent came up at work. He has to go to a meeting in the office. There is a minute of relief in that thought followed by an all new, more compelling one, a realization that he can't go home without knowing what is going on with the boy, the kid with the strange name, Ibram. Lewis is actually scared. Feels a shiver. Then, in a moment of deadened senses, he sets his drink aside and stretches out on the old man's manly leather sofa, so comfortable and accepting of his weight.

～

It is nearly ten o'clock when he leaves the house and drives across town to the hospital, prodded by the old man's top shelf bourbon that he's been drinking under the front porch light infested with circling moths, and dressed in the suit and tie he had packed in case there was a funeral. Now it is a uniform, a costume that he hopes will make him look serious, a figure of some authority.

The parking lot is all but empty and dimly lit, like there are no muggers or thieves in this town and never will be. The lights at the entrance are brighter and some of the windows on the upper floors are lit, which gives some sort of permission to leave this dark, sick world and go into one that is supposed to offer help. There is a nice lobby, a few people in a waiting area, including an old man with a pot of bright red geraniums sitting in his lap. No one is at the reception counter, only a sign-up sheet on a clipboard. He signs a fake name in a scrawl and ignores the column that asks for the time.

In the hallway, at the elevators, a man running a mop back and forth over the tile floor glances up and then ignores him. He takes the elevator one level up and walks the length of the corridor, hoping there will be a friendly nurse. He'll say that he's been visiting a friend, was just leaving, and then causally ask about the boy in the newspaper, a boy his son went to school with. Two elderly women on walkers raise their heads and smile. An empty nurses' station and a few visitors in an alcove.

At the end of the corridor, he takes stairs to the second floor. There, not far from the stairway, behind well-marked double doors, is the entrance to the ICU and a warning, Do Not Enter. Here, the lights are lower than on the floor below. It's terribly quiet and the air a bit medicinal. He stands planted for a moment trying to imagine what might be going on in there, behind the secret door. All at once, he comes back to himself, the urgency to get done what he's come to do, then fly home, putting a thousand miles between himself and this place. Closing his eyes, Lewis sees a trim lawn and then his small office in a bright corner of his house. The moment passes. He lets out a warm breath, feeling a little lighter on his feet.

A bit consoled that he's made an honest effort, he starts to leave down the stairwell and would have if not for a light spilling onto the floor halfway down the corridor. The light comes from a small alcove. It is a waiting area and seated on a sofa against the far wall are a man and woman. The man is stout with a neatly trimmed beard and shoulders that seem capable of lifting just about anything he cared to lift, and the woman is thin in a nice dress, with thick, bushy African hair. On the floor in front of them, a little girl is sleeping on a folded blanket with one hand tucked under her head. Toys lie around her, crayons, a stack of books, and a black doll in a gauzy blue dress decorated with tiny sequins. When Lewis finally steps into the light, the mother leans forward, touches the girl, and moves the doll a little closer, like that might help her sleep better.

Unprepared for this and not sure what to hope for, Lewis loosens his tie, sits down, and leans forward, placing his head in his hands. Gazing at his shoes, he works to find words for these people that will come out sounding the way he wants them to. Finally, he raises his head.

"Oh, man," he utters, speaking across the little girl, "long night, huh. My wife, she's down the hall having a baby, or trying to, she's having a rough time of it right now. Hell, all this waiting."

"My, I'm sorry," the woman says. "Surely things'll work out for her. They have good doctors here."

"Actually," Lewis says, "we're not from here. We're visiting her mother and at supper she started having contractions and it's more than a month before she's due."

"A month is okay," the woman says.

Lewis glances at the girl. "You've got a pretty little girl. What's her name?"

The man touches his wife's arm. He sits up. "Sofiya," he says.

"We call her Sofi," the woman says.

"Sofiya, that's a nice name. A nice name to take through life." Awkward words that bring no response. Lewis shifts in the chair and, hoping to keep things going, mentions his work, manufacturing, he says, small appliances mostly, and describes how he is working while he's here, remote, by computer.

Then, he asks the man, "What do you do?"

"Do?"

"He means work."

"I know what he means. I'm at the city. I keep the water pumps going."

"Water pumps?"

"Pumps and mains and piping and all."

"That sounds like an engineer."

"He's in charge of it," the woman says, "all the water." She has lovely teeth, straight, pearly when she opens her mouth. She's wearing soft pink lipstick.

"It's good water," Lewis goes on. "I'll vouch for that. Here, we drink it straight out of the tap. Better than what we have back east."

Reaching his phone from his coat pocket, Lewis pretends to check for messages. When he glances up, the woman is watching him and he notices her eyes, realizing that never before in the thirty-eight years of his life has he looked into the eyes of a black woman. Hers aren't as dark as he might have expected. They are a warm shade of brown, like chestnuts, perfectly clear and serious below her lashes. And he knows beyond doubt that they are connecting and that coming here, finding out about the boy, showing respect for him, is a godsend, exactly what he needed to do.

He says, "We've been here a couple of weeks now and I've been reading the newspaper. This morning, there was a story about an accident downtown. A boy involved. I was just wondering if by chance you might know about him."

"Know?" the man said.

"I mean, if that's why you all are here?"

"Yes, he's ours," the woman says, as if there was something final about it.

"Oh, man. I'm sorry to hear that, really sorry. I hope he's doing ok."

The man starts to speak, but his wife breaks in. "He is going to be fine. They're taking good care of him and we're waiting right now for a new doctor to come in, a specialist."

"That's good news," Lewis says. "The paper mentioned something about his legs."

"We're praying, and a lot of people are, too, and he's strong and going to be fine."

"I have a friend," Lewis says, "a great old friend who's in the medical field, and I can tell you from what he tells me that the treatment and machines they have these days are unbelievable."

The father stands up. His face changes, a smile appears, slight, but real. And at once, a group of women arrive. Three women in dresses or skirts are suddenly filling up the small space, and for the next minute or so there is a quiet shower of greetings, kisses, and hugs. One of the women, quite large, tugs at her dark dress, bends over, and touches the sleeping girl, runs her hand over her hair as if offering a blessing. *Grandmother*, Lewis's mind says. He is standing like the rest of them, breathing in the fresh scent of perfumes or colognes that has descended over the room, and preparing himself to react to whatever might happen next.

Once they all find places to sit, he sits down as well. One of the women, the smallest of the three, wearing a skirt that goes almost to the floor, is carrying a large tote bag with a splash of yellow flowers embroidered on it. While they talk with each other in low voices, speaking of people and occurrences Lewis knows nothing about, the tote bag is opened. Two thermos bottles come out, napkins, small paper plates, a fat paper bag.

"We got hot tea and coffee," one of the women announces; the oldest of the bunch, she carries a shiny black cane.

"And cake donuts," the small woman adds. Cups appear and steaming drinks are poured. The woman with the cane looks over at Lewis. "We've got coffee here," she says, and without another word, pours coffee into a blue ceramic mug, comes over on stout, uncertain legs, and puts it in Lewis's hands.

"This one's for Sofi," the grandmother says, placing a donut on a paper plate. They all sit back with their coffee or their tea and watch while the woman gently wakes her granddaughter, helps her sit up straight, and places the paper plate with the donut on it in her lap. Then, as if drawn to a performance, they all watch the girl, her large, gleaming eyes blinking at first and then opening wide. She glances back at her mother and then looks around the room as if to assess the situation and begins nibbling at the donut. A few crumbs fall and then more, until, with everyone delighted, smiling, the girl's eyes close and her head drops. Her mother steadies her as she topples over and slowly stretches out on the blanket just as before.

The coffee is steaming, strong, slightly bitter, but as welcome as any cup of coffee Lewis has ever had. Looking around the room, he raises the cup. "Thank you all for this. I needed it, who the hell wants to drink coffee out of a machine."

"We got plenty of donuts," the mother says to him. "It looks like Sofi's not going to eat hers."

There are chuckles, glances at the girl, at each other.

It goes on, Lewis sipping the coffee trying to keep up appearances. "This ought to keep a person awake," he says. And they surely hear him, but there's no response and as his words drift away, the group of them turn inward to address each other, lights attached to the walls sufficient to create weak shadows and illuminate the father's close-cropped hair. Finally, they begin discussing the condition of the boy, speaking in grave and hopeful generalities, assurances, relieved at what the mother tells them about the new doctor, the tubes and devices already unhooked from the boy, the way he has a bit of an appetite, optimism from one of the nurses, and the prognosis they had gotten just a while ago.

Lewis sits as a spectator outside of the circle, even as the father tells the women what he has learned about the accident, what the police said, promises there would be an investigation, requests for patience. And all along, while caught in the rhythm of his words, Lewis can see in clear details what they have no way of seeing—the harsh sunlight, sudden dash off the curb, cars breaking and a loud crash driving the pickup forward, shocked faces. It scares him to know so much when these people, who have a claim on the boy, are so blind, and still Lewis holds his tongue stiff in his mouth, protecting himself, the only person on earth who knows and hopefully will ever know exactly what had taken place—the deceit of it all something like a snake ready to bite.

When the parents' story has ended and enough time has passed for everyone to take it in and contemplate it, the mother turns her eyes on Lewis.

"Listen," she says to the others and tells them about his wife, her struggle to give birth in a strange place. From all around come looks of compassion and simple words of encouragement, sympathy that, for a moment, seems to alter the quality of the air in the room.

"Thank you all," Lewis manages to get out. "I'll tell her." And then, desperate to change the subject, to separate himself from the lies surrounding him, he asks the first thing that comes into his head, were they all related.

"Well, you could say that," the one who had brought the coffee says after a pause. "We're all related by the church."

"Isn't that the truth," the grandmother says. "The whole truth when you consider what matters. In my mind right now," she goes on, "it's past time for us to stand together and offer up a prayer. Look now, everybody gather 'round here," she announces, standing and holding out her heavy arms. One by one, they rise and quietly form a circle in front of the sleeping girl. Once they are in place, the grandmother asks Lewis to join them, her eyes telling him he has no choice.

"Now, you come on," the woman with the cane says and the circle opens, and she runs her arm through Lewis's arm, pulls him tight against her. The father looks across at Lewis, not smiling but not hostile either. Heads are lowered, each one in turn, and the grandmother draws a breath, closes her eyes, and prays for Ibram, a short prayer full of warmth and confidence and spiritual praise. Then, as her voice trails off, she turns to Lewis. "Your wife," she says to him, "we'll pray a prayer for her, too. What's her name?"

Her name? A black hole opens in Lewis's mind. He struggles to bring up his wife's name, but there is no way he can utter it, bring her presence into this room. Other names follow, but none of them sound real to him. The woman holding his arm squeezes tighter and his eyes close the way those old dolls' closed, when their heads were tilted back, and in his blindness, Lewis hears the grandmother's voice. "That's all right," she says. "It doesn't matter. We'll offer the prayer and God will put the name in."

Arlene and Ell

Arlene had taken a place up front just behind the driver where she gazed out of the rain-streaked window, the big trucks going by lighting up her face. She looked tired. We were all pretty beat up. Seven shows in five cities in nine days, a pace that was going to go on for the next few weeks. It was after two by the time we got the gear packed up and stowed away, the five of us humping it with a small local stage crew and cold blasts of wind howling through the alley behind the Tower Theater. Nobody complaining, just get it done and into the warm bus and dry clothes and on the road out of Oklahoma City, so we'd get some sleep and make it to Boulder with time to relax before setting up for the next show. After Boulder, it would be Boise and then Twin Falls and then on to Reno for a few days which is as much of the calendar as I had in my head at that time.

Once through downtown and onto I-70, we warmed up some chili and made sandwiches and ate and drank some and smoked some. As I said, there were five of us in the band, which was put together by Arlene and her manager, who had the idea of creating a mixed group, white, black, Hispanic, male, female. We had been together eight or nine months by then and this was our first tour and it seemed to be going well. Arlene played bass and Violeta drums and percussion. Having women in those roles definitely added to the aesthetics. What's more, we were an older bunch, not one of us under fifty, Arlene fifty-seven and me some years ahead of her. We had all been in the business for a lot of years and had friends in common and some recognition and were getting along okay career wise. Nobody tried to hog the stage or bitched about playing each other's songs or covering particular old standards, though there were some signs of jockeying around now that we had been approached by a producer who was talking about an album.

Anyway, everybody had gone to bed except Arlene. I had woken up, which was my habit after an hour's sleep, and gone up front and observed her absorbed in whatever was outside the bus until she looked up like she knew I'd been standing there waiting like an old tramp in front of a store window. "If you can't sleep, how about making coffee," she said. "That would be good, don't you think."

And so I went back and made coffee and put cups and the pot on a tray and brought it out. She set up the hideaway table and we sat across from one another other with our coffee not saying much. "Are you writing anything?" I asked, fed up with the quiet, and she said, "I'm not ready to show it," and I could see she was feeling a little testy.

"Sorry, but I was thinking about home," she said then, putting her cup down. "I mean home where I was a kid." I knew she had grown up in West Texas. "Lubbock?" I asked that because some good musicians had come from there and it was the first town I thought of. "No, I grew up in a smaller place. Childress. It's just a few hours south of here."

"You miss it sometimes?" I asked her, and about that time Violeta came out, bringing her own cup. A pretty woman, stout like a wrestler and long, shimmering black hair that a girl a third her age would be proud of. She was wearing black knit pants and a sweatshirt. We were all dressed warm because keeping the thermostat low was better for sleeping. Violeta sat down next to me. I poured coffee. "We're talking about home," I told her. "I mean our real home, where we grew up." "I'm lucky," she said. "When this trip's done, I'll be going there with Mark." Mark was her husband, a retired high school principal who ran a youth shelter now. "We're spending a week with our kids and grandkids and then going to Miami for a while, just the two of us."

"You got family there?" "Nobody, that's the reason we're going," she laughed, her eyes sparkling.

Before long, I put my cup down and started to get up to leave them alone. They enjoyed each other's company. "You know, I've been thinking," Arlene said, all at once. "I'd like to tell you two a story." "About home?" Violeta asked her. "Yeah, partly. Actually, it's something I've never told anybody. Not my parents or brothers or my first husband or second—and there won't be a third one," she glanced at me, a clear message. "In any case," she said, "for me it's personal and a ghost story too, I guess you could call it." She pressed her lips together and glanced at each of us and then opened her lovely mouth and started out.

"When I first began playing," she said, "I was hardly ten years old. My parents aren't particularly musical, but there was a high school boy down the road named Eddie Perez, who had a garage band, only his garage was an old horse barn down a dirt trail behind his house. I'd walk by and hear the music coming out of there and one day got up the nerve to step on the path and keep walking. I think they were happy to have somebody listening, even if it was a skinny little tomboy. I kept showing up and on weekends sometimes bringing a friend or two with me. Before long, I was telling myself I can do that and was dying to get my hands on a guitar. Eddie was a smart, happy kid. He played the bass and one afternoon strapped it on me. God it was heavy, but I loved it the second I started picking the steel strings. His dad was quite a player, respected in West Texas, and he and Eddie, seeing how thrilled and serious I was, offered lessons but tried to get me to switch to guitar because they said women didn't play bass. But I wouldn't have it and finally they gave in. Pretty soon, I was picking out some songs and then learning cords and, in time, outlining notes. In my wild head, it seemed I had found nirvana, though, of course, I couldn't have guessed what nirvana might be like.

"After a while, my parents bought me a decent second-hand Hi-Flier and Eddie's dad loaned me an amp he didn't intend to get back. From then on, I practiced every day and often played with Eddie's group as well. My first year in high school, I put together a little band, three of us and then four. We got popular enough to play at school dances in our town and then towns around, even if it was a long drive, which is the case in West Texas. We played at livestock shows and county fairs and flea markets and places like that. Sometimes Dad and Mom would come and film us with a little eight-millimeter camera. Dad's first cousin Floyd was a bartender in New Orleans, a singer also, and deep into the music scene there. Dad sent him a reel and he phoned and asked for more of them. Cousin Floyd's family lived in Fort Worth and one day when he was visiting his parents, he drove up to spend the night and watch us play.

"He told me the band wasn't much, but I had talent and, he said, a stage presence, which shook me enough to kept me up at night. 'Stay with it,' he told me, 'being a girl on bass, you might find a niche.' The spring just before I graduated, he called and said 'Come down here and I'll teach you to tend bar,' which was a valuable skill for anybody who was serious about playing music. It was a month of turmoil between me and my parents, but an eighteen-year-old girl who can't wrap her dad around her little finger isn't worth her salt.

"By then, I had a green Ford pickup I was in love with. The body was pretty rough and it rattled, but who'd want an old pickup that didn't rattle, and it ran well. Mom and Dad bought a new set of tires. My brother and I tuned it up, replaced the belts and hoses and early on a Sunday morning, I started out for New Orleans."

Arlene sighed, got up, and walked the aisle up and back, to catch her breath, I guess. It was raining hard now, the rain pounding like it was determined to tear through the roof. Horton, our driver, slowed down to a crawl. I stuck my head past the partition. "You doing okay," I asked him. "No problem," he said. "Fresh coffee?" I asked and he handed me his thermos.

"Ask Arlene if there's more to the story," he said to me when I got back with his coffee. Arlene piped up. "I'm just getting started," and soon went on.

"I've never thought much about fate," she said, "but if I hadn't set off without checking the gas gage, none of this would have happened. Half an hour down the road, I realized I was low on gas and limped into a truck stop. I recall creeping past a line of big eighteen-wheelers, feeling like a bug about to be stepped on. I'm sure you know what I mean. Anyway, when I left, the eastern sky was bright orange and the sun was rising in my face, so I nearly missed her, a woman standing beside the on-ramp with her thumb out. Despite it being July, she had on a long coat and carried a small suitcase. Of course, I knew better than to pick up a hitch-hiker and tried to creep on past, but my heart spoke up and I couldn't help myself. Better I pick her up than let some asshole do it.

"I stopped and backed up. She shoved the suitcase into the truck bed, opened the door, pushed my bass case aside, and climbed in at the same time I was trying to ask her where she was going.

'All the way home,' she said, settling in.

'Where's that?'

'Well, Sour Springs,' she said, like I should already know that.

"Because of what would happen, I'm tempted to say she seemed witchy, but she didn't. She was old, short, broad, a small, round head that sat on her shoulders so she had hardly any neck. Her hair was streaked gray and white, nicely braided and wrapped around her head and fixed with a clip. A wide mouth and narrow eyes like she could have been part Indian or even Chinese.

"I told her I was going to New Orleans.

'That's fine,' she said, 'Sour Springs will get you there. I'll show you.'

"With her coat open, I saw she was clutching a big purse against her chest. Of course, I was beginning to get nervous, thinking what the hell have I gotten myself into.

"I've got a map." I told her.

'No need. I know the roads.' She tapped her forehead.

"I told her the coat would be hot. I didn't have any air conditioner."

"She said nothing.

"Against my will, I took my bass and settled it in the truck bed against the cab, protected by a duffel bag and cardboard boxes my mother had helped me pack, things I'd need if I was going to live alone. My passenger's cheap little suitcase was tucked away in a corner.

"Back in the truck, I tried again to get her to take off the coat but nothing doing.

"Already screaming at myself, I nearly caused a wreck getting onto the highway. This wasn't the trip I'd planned. I was counting on solitude, the excitement of contemplating a new existence, singing at the top of my lungs if I wanted to. Instead, she sat there like a stump with deep roots. She picked up my water jar, unscrewed the top, and took a long drink, at least a quart went down her throat, and I began to plan how I was ever going to get rid of her.

"I felt the need to assert myself and so told her outright that she ought to know better than to be hitchhiking, that it was dangerous for a woman. 'I couldn't say,' she said, 'I never did it before.' Sometime later, just outside of Wichita Falls, she spoke up again and told me to turn off this highway as soon as I could. Then, she repeated herself. 'There's going to be a jam up,' she said. A few minutes later, the cars ahead of us were slowing down and then we were crawling along, stopping, starting. We passed a patrol car, a wrecker, a semi, and battered cars on the shoulder. Firemen were hosing down the highway. All of this the first sign of something that I didn't allow myself to think about.

"Once we were past the mess, the old woman wiggled out of her coat, folded it into a thick cushion, sat on top of it in a long dark dress, and gazed out of the windshield like the captain of a boat. 'Perk up before Fort Worth,' she told me. 'I'll show you the way around.'

"Like you can imagine, I was going nuts. The sun was up and beginning to blaze and sweat already soaked my shirt. 'If I could, I'd do some driving,' she told me. 'My husband did the driving when we had something to drive other than a wagon.' She asked my name. I said nothing, thinking I would give a big toe for a radio right then.

"In a while, though, I relented and told her."

'They named me Elleen,' she said, 'but you call me Ell.'

"I told her I'd never heard that name."

'It ain't common. But there are others where I come from.'

"When the tall buildings of downtown Fort Worth came into view across the prairie, she began to give me directions. The cautious part of my mind wanted to argue, but I couldn't find the words, maybe because she'd been right once already and, also, I had no experience driving in a big city. We took one road after another, all the while circling the tall downtown buildings.

"When the city was finally behind us, we were on a four-lane highway going more or less south by my calculations and I began to realize that something was wrong. We were supposed to be headed east toward Dallas, that's the way my dad and I had marked it on the map. And I told her so. 'Nope,' she said, like there wasn't any reason to consider it.

"We crossed a river. There was a rest area and I pulled off, reached the map out of the glove compartment and went to a picnic table and laid it out. Sure enough, the pencil line went straight through Fort Worth to Dallas and on the far side of Dallas, southeast. She wouldn't have it. 'We're due in Sour Springs this evening,' she told me. 'No time to dawdle.' I told her there was no Sour Springs on the map, that I'd given it a careful search. 'Don't matter,' she said, 'my husband'll be waiting for us and then it's easy for you on to Louisiana.' The fact is, her will was stronger than mine.

"Once we were on the road again, I told her I wanted to get a coke and go to the ladies. I pulled off into the first gas station, stopped by the pumps, and left her in the truck. When I came out of the restroom door, she was waiting there, hugging her purse, and without a word, went straight in. No wonder, because by that time, she had drank both of my water jars dry. Anyway, I saw my chance, jumped, ran to the truck, and grabbed her suitcase, which was light as a feather. I ran back and dropped it on the counter, telling the clerk to give it to the old lady when she came out of the restroom.

"I ran back, started the engine, and nearly ran over her. She was standing square in front of the truck, looking through the windshield straight into my eyes. I can't explain how she could have gotten there that fast. It's beyond explanation or maybe a trick of time it would take Einstein to figure out. She put the suitcase in the bed and climbed in, clutching her purse.

"By then, I can tell you I was confused and pretty much worn out, even a little shaky, disconcerted. My mind wasn't capable of telling me what to do next. What I did was ask her if she wanted a coke because I did. 'I don't drink nothing but water,' she said. I went in and bought a coke, some chocolate bars, and filled the water jugs.

"We were half an hour down the road when, in a soft, firm voice that didn't allow for objections, she told me to turn off this highway. We were soon on a farm to market road going east or nearly so. You'd think I'd be depleted by this time, but just the opposite. Too tensed up, riled up, curious, or maybe on a sugar high, I can't say, but I remember slowly realizing that at some point a line had been crossed and Ell was in my life and would be till she was where she wanted to be.

"Even so, it was a nice country road. There were big, green hardwood trees, green farmland, crops, milk cows—things you're not used to where I was from. A large brown hawk or maybe an eagle sat on a telephone pole, watching the sky like something interesting would be coming along any minute now.

"In a small town, we stopped at a Dairy Queen and sat inside, shivering under the air-conditioner. The woman behind the counter brought our hamburgers to the table. 'That your granddaughter?' she asked Ell. 'I can see the resemblance.'

'People see what they want to see,' Ell said bluntly. Which shocked the woman into a frown.

"I had brought my bass in for safety's sake. The woman turned to me, 'you play that?'

"I took the bass out of the case to show it to her, or really to show Ell, and was soon telling her about my music and why I was on the way to New Orleans. I guess it was the first time I'd ever used music to define myself to anyone."

Arlene paused a minute, her face a little flushed. The rain was now so slow you had to strain your ears to hear it coming down on the roof of the bus.

"I remember it was a hot day," Arlene went on. "The road wind blowing through the truck windows was like something coming out of a furnace and Ell perched on her cushion reminded me of an old owl that might spread her wings and fly out of there at any minute. We drank water, passing the jar back and forth. I would ask her a question about herself and when I saw she was reticent, went on talking about myself, which was unusual, at least back then at that age."

And still is, I broke in.

"It could be you don't ask the right questions at the right time," Arlene said.

"A major problem with men," Violeta spoke up, turning her eyes at me. Arlene emitted a smile. I grabbed the pot and went back to make fresh coffee.

"What she told me," Arlene said, when I got back, "is that where she came from, people didn't care for people talking about themselves, but she would tell what she could as long as it came out right. She leaned over and set her purse on the floorboard, the first time she had let go of it, I think.

'I'm one-fourth Alabama-Coushatta,' she said, 'born on the edge of the reservation is how people used to describe it. I grew up quick in a good family of seven children but got married at an ancient age, twenty-five. My husband is James Peete and he was thirty-two, had gone to the war and stayed on some years in the army before coming back home. He had some money in the bank and a little pension from a war wound, but that wasn't it. I'd turned down several, but he was the one for me, otherwise I'd have never married.

'We bought some land near Sour Springs and added to it. We had a nice cedar-plank house, farmed, and kept an orchard, chickens, range cattle, and hogs. In those days, there wasn't hardly any fence in the thickets and farmers let their cattle run wherever they wanted no matter whose property it was. Cattle would mostly forage and take care of themselves until you got ready to bring them in, which required the help of dogs and we had two good ones. When we needed something extra, we would sell timber to a sawmill. The woods at the back of our property grew the biggest loblolly pines you can imagine. James, who's a big man, couldn't reach halfway around the biggest ones.

'I was thirty when we finally got pregnant. It was a boy. We named him James Junior and called him J.J. He was a darling but born with afflictions in his body and later on we found in his mind as well. There's a name for it, but saying it out loud would make me start cussing. He would never learn to walk properly or talk properly and took a lot of taking care of. James adored him and we taught him to do more for himself than the doctors thought he would ever be capable of. On the other hand, he never lacked for anything that could be humanly provided.'

"While Ell went on talking, we passed through a prosperous looking small town, reached a crossroads, and turned right going south. From then on, every turn took us onto a rougher and narrower road. The woods grew thicker, darker, and in some parts swampy, it seemed, though I'd never seen anything like a swamp in my life. At times, you'd think the sun was an afterthought.

"After a long time on a dirt road, we came to a certain wooden bridge over a creek and she told me to stop. 'Right there,' she said, pointing upstream, 'is where I was baptized. I was ten years old,' she said. She opened the door, slid out, and I parked the truck off the road and followed her through a jungle of big palmetto palms down to the creek. The creek was wide and slow and the woods so quiet your ears hurt.

'I know what you been wanting to get at,' she said to me once we had sat down on the bank. 'You wonder why I want to come back here, nearly broke, no change of clothes, hitching a ride, don't you.

For one thing, buses don't come anywhere near here and, anyway, I had faith you'd be coming along.'

"She said the minute she saw me and got into the truck, she felt it, but once I had tried to run away at the gas station and wasn't able to, she was sure of it. Then all at once, she raised her palm, calling for quiet. I closed my mouth and before long, the silence was broken by the sound of birds singing. After a minute or so, there was a crow cutting through the music...*caw, caw, caw.* 'There it is,' she said, as if she'd been expecting it, and closed her eyes. I wondered if she was praying or maybe in pain because that's what I saw in her face, something troubling.

"It lasted a few minutes, the total silence, but once recovered, she relaxed and opened up again. She said that on J.J.'s thirteenth birthday, her husband came down with a fever due to the frost and cold rains that winter, in conjunction with his war wound, a slice of iron that had likely been leaking poison all those years. He developed a cough that turned to flu and then to what she called lung fever, worse than consumption, she said. One day while James was sick in bed, a man came around wanting to buy timber. He had seen their big pine trees. He named a low price and her husband sent him packing. Soon, he came back with another man and James sent them off together.

"At the same time, he was getting worse and when the doctor finally had him taken to a hospital, she knew he wouldn't be coming back. It was hard to explain to J.J. and in the end even harder on him than it was on her. In time, the hospital bill came and there was no way to pay except with the timber. But when she went out to survey the trees, all she found was open sky and tall stumps. To make the work fast and easy, they had cut the trees waist-high. What's more, they took the small ones as well. Left nothing. They had taken advantage of James' death and had no conscience except almighty greed, she said, turning her small hands into bony fists.

"The law and lawyers got involved. Things dragged on and as you can imagine, the farm started going downhill. She couldn't take care of it and J.J., too. Her sister who lived in West Texas offered to take them in. 'Bless her and her cowboy husband,' she said.

"By this time, Ell had taken on a terribly solemn demeanor. I wanted to help, but in my sheltered life had had little experience with grief or the words to express comfort and so gazed across the creek and waited. After a while, she hauled herself up and said, 'Well come on.' I followed her along the creek and we came to a path that lead off into the trees. 'Wild hog trail,' she said, and asked if I had ever heard of a mud boil and, of course, I hadn't.

"We took the trail through thick bush and vines to a small pond or pit that was out of some prehistoric era. The thing was really pure mud bubbling and boiling like a soup cooking, even though it was cool to the touch, I'm not kidding you. She told me her people said it was the devil breathing and she said the words for it in their language.

"While we stood there, she offered another story that I now assume, from what she would tell me later, is the sort of haunted witchery that she believed in. Back during the Civil War, she said, turncoats and soldiers deserted from the Rebel army would run away and hide in the swamps and thickets around there. When the regulars rooted one out, they would cut off his head and hang it from a limb. At night you could see those heads lit up like lanterns.

"I can't say how seriously she believed those things but that walk into the woods seemed to have revived her. The next time she opened up we were far down the road. By then, it was moving toward evening and the shadows of trees passing over us. Ell took a long drink of water and then in a calm, careful voice told me that a month ago, the seventeenth day of June, J.J. had passed out of this world. At the same time, she said, James passed back into it. She first glimpsed him at the burial. He stood at their son's gravesite with his head bowed, wearing a felt hat that he once owned and the suitcoat he was buried in. He never looked at her, just appeared for a minute and vanished. 'For the next few weeks, I'd dream him up in my sleep,' she said, 'and she understood without hearing words that he and J.J. were waiting for her and also brooding over the trees that had been stolen off their land.

"Your pine trees?" I asked her.

'I don't normally talk about revenge,' she said, 'too often it'll come back on you, but with the time I have left, I'm not worried about it. James is going to put a curse on them thieves, a hex, something auspicious, so they'll suffer worse than we suffered,' she said, patting the purse, as if something I didn't need to know about was in there waiting to come out. 'I got what he asked for right here.'

"Naturally, that blew my mind. On the other hand, it was so absurd there was nothing to say. Has she totally lost it, I wondered, and then I thought, no, she's just trying to shock me or entertain herself and me and keep me driving, even if she seemed dead serious. Whatever, thoughts like those helped keep me steady and my nerves sane enough, even while evening was coming down.

"For a while, no words left her lips or mine. She drank water. I didn't dare touch it. I turned all my heart and energy toward driving, putting faith in my truck to get me where I needed to be. We made two or three more turns, the last one onto a dirt lane. We went up a long hill that ended in front of a small, white church with a steeple and beyond it was a cemetery. She directed me to drive up to the entrance, which included an overhead trellis covered in vines with white flowers. Beyond it, tombstones set in a random fashion disappeared into the dark under big trees.

'I'll be leaving you here,' Ell said, and she then gave me directions, which she said would take me across the river into Louisiana and then to the doorstep of New Orleans. A hop and a jump, she said. She climbed out with her bag, put on her long coat, got her suitcase from the truck bed, and came back to my window. 'By the weekend, you'll be in a fine place playing your guitar,' she said, 'I can promise that,' and without another word, turned and walked through the entrance into the trees, offering no goodbye or even a word of thanks."

Arlene stopped there, her words hanging in air. Feeling uncertain, I might have tried saying something smart and funny, lightened things up. Instead, I ran some words through my head and said out loud, "Okay, if you consider it for minute, it can probably be explained logically," which was definitely the wrong response. The two of them looked at me with identical expressions, like I'd spoken out of turn or, worse, committed some kind of blasphemy. And to my credit, I got it this time—keep your thoughts to yourself, this is something between women. In any case, without remarks from Violeta, Arlene said that there was a little more. And in a minute, she took up where she had left off.

"You both know it was more than a hop and jump," she said, "and for the first part of the drive, at least until I crossed over the Sabine River, I'd glance at the seat next to me expecting to see her. I felt empty, solemn, wondering how in god's name she could be real and not a figment and next wondering what was happening to her at that minute. With one stop for gas, I got to New Orleans just an hour later than expected, ten o'clock. At a gas station, I phoned Cousin Floyd at the bar and he came and took me to his place, which was in an old neighborhood a few blocks from the French Quarter. His wife hugged me at the door and his little boy came in rubbing his eyes and hugged me also. Two days later, I started behind the bar. It was a popular place with a long bar and a restaurant and a stage back in one corner. There was a house band and others played there at times. I started out pulling beers and in a few days was mixing drinks.

"On Saturday, my shift started at noon. Floyd came in later. He told me that the band's bass player had broken his wrist. It was in a cast. Was I up for an audition, which, of course, set my brain on fire. I could've screamed. He gave me an address and I ran to his house for my bass and, swimming in sweat, caught a taxi for the first time ever. Dave Chilton, the bass player, was an electrician by trade and he took me behind his house to a shed filled with electrical and music equipment. He was a chunky guy with a mustache and hair like Elvis Presley. He listened to me play what I wanted for a few minutes. Then, he wrote out a list of songs the band was likely to play that night. I had played a few of them and heard nearly all of the others. I chose one and played it along with a tape going in the background, amazed at how the sound resonated on his amp as compared to my cheap one. It pumped me with confidence and he let me play pieces of a few more songs. Finally, he said, 'This bunch is easy to play with. Stay close to the piano, just keep the rhythm, hang back when you need to. Don't play when you're not sure and don't get fancy.' A guy with a bright white cast on his lower arm and wrist and definitely high, maybe on painkillers and something else too. 'Okay, gal, you'll have to do,' he finally said to me, words I'd remember for the rest of my life.

"The place was packed. The band was courteous, loose. We started playing at ten. At first my fingers were sweating on the pick, but I kept my eyes off the audience, settled down, and it went well. In fact, playing with real players lifted me up, even if I was impressing no one but myself. Ell never entered my mind until late the next morning. And, in the heat, I went down through Jackson Square and sat on the levee above the Mississippi and marveled at what she'd done for me."

The Chinquapin Tree

Glancing out of the kitchen window this morning, I caught sight of Ellie, my ten-year-old, chasing a cotton-headed boy named Benny Fayette across our mowed pasture and into the orchard my husband and I have been tending since we moved into this place. I'm sure most people would say it was innocent child play, as natural as morning sunlight. But watching the two of them expending so much wild, careless energy prompted memories I had been trying to foreswear for a very long time.

On this day, rather than ignore them as I was liable to do, I made a cup of black tea and went out onto our back patio and in the warm morning sun, sat down right in the middle of them. As I began to relax, a strange thought occurred, a totally new one; if I'd let myself, I could surely blame everything on the tree. It was a chinquapin tree and it seemed a miracle to see one that big hidden away in the woods, like what in the world would ever have put it there.

This was more than twenty years ago. I'd turned fourteen, about to start high school. He was a somewhat short, hefty boy a year or so older than me, Gil McDaniel. After school that fall, a group of us would often come off the bus, drop our books, and run out through an open field of bluestem and Indian grass on into the woods and thickets beyond our houses. We would climb trees and swing on vines and saplings, invent games, gather wild pears from stunted trees that managed to grow there just for us, we thought.

This time, a brisk, gray afternoon, there was only Gil and me. I don't recall why the others went straight back home except that it was a somewhat dreary day, the sky hung with dark patches of clouds and a little windy as if a norther might be coming in. The two of us crossed the paved road, dropped our books in the grass, and took off over the field through a sagging barbed-wire fence and into the trees. Farther on, there was a long slope crossed with eroded gullies and patches of hardwoods and saplings where we would usually stop and start our games. But this day, Gil and I went on over a trickling, no name creek and deeper into the woods. The leaves were turning red and yellow and, running through the ones covering the ground, you'd kick them up, making a racket. Gil was a good runner, though a little awkward like he had a naturally stiff knee or one leg might be a bit shorter than the other one. That and his smooth, pale-freckled face and sharp brown eyes is what I mostly recall about his appearance.

"My brother showed me a chinquapin tree you wouldn't believe," he'd told me that morning on the school grounds, reaching his arms into a big half-circle. "The biggest chinquapin you ever seen."

"Saw," I scolded.

And he spit and chased me back into the school building.

Anyway, when we finally reached the tree, it was exactly as he had described, exactly that big. So much of it it seemed to dominate everything else around it. A rough, thick trunk and wild grapevines the size of a young boy's arm trailing up through the branches toward the sky. In other words, a tree worth bragging about, one that begged to be climbed.

He went up first on a vine, hand over hand and kicking his legs, which is the way he climbed, the way boys liked to climb, showing off their strength, until he was deep into the leaves and branches nearly out of sight. I dropped my sandals and tugged my skirt straight—not the ideal garment for climbing—and went up like I knew how to, using my bare feet on the trunk, pulling on vines with my arms, and then bending through the limbs and branches to catch him near the top. From up there, we seemed to be halfway to the sky, the moving, gray clouds changing shape. Out on the highway that went into town, you could see cars and trucks going by, cattle in a distant pasture, and the Eason's little roan filly in some kind of excitement, running along a fence line.

It was peaceful. I was taken with it, a new view of the world I knew so well, now much more beautiful and orderly, plots of land arranged in patterns like an easy jigsaw puzzle. After a minute or so, I realized Gil had moved close to me. He reached and grasped my wrist and then his breath was on my face. He leaned in, trying to kiss me, which was a complete surprise, and scary, partly because I was suddenly off balance. He said my name in a voice I hardly recognized. It wasn't that I hadn't been kissed before, but it had always been in a game or gentle and quick and over with. His voice told me that he wanted something else. When I didn't respond, he suddenly grabbed a fistful of my hair.

"Gil, let go," I let out. "You're hurting me," I said. "I'm getting dizzy." I said *please* and then, with little choice, let him put his mouth against my dry lips. He released my hair. I turned away and started scrambling down one limb to the next until I found a vine and swung out, burning my hands as I slid to ground.

By the time my feet were under me, Gil was there, too.

He grabbed my shoulders, digging in his fingers. I shook my head, telling him that I didn't want to...I'd had enough. He kept talking in a voice I hardly recognized and then in one quick motion, kicked my feet out from under me. I hit the ground hard, flat on my back. We burrowed into the rotting leaves, wrestling, me already short of breath. Somehow, he yanked my skirt up over my head. In the darkness under the skirt, I felt his forearm press into my throat until I was suffocating. He continued pressing into my windpipe and, nearly paralyzed, I got scared of being hurt and made a conscious decision to stop fighting, to become a possum, and I went limp, amazed at how much stronger he was than me. His hands roamed over my body, yanked at my panties. I waited. He was huffing in a scary way, shoving against me. Then, after a long minute, nothing. He stopped. I felt him roll off of me.

When I pulled my skirt back down, he was standing nearby buckling his belt, looking down, a towering figure it seemed. "Don't tell nobody," he said, and said it again. Then, his voice was softer. "Promise. You got to promise," he said.

And so, I did. I promised and meant it, crying a little. I didn't want anyone to know any more than he did. I suppose he would have been aware of that. The truth is, at that time, I knew less about sex than some others my age. Of course, I had secretly experimented, but otherwise it wasn't in my vocabulary except as jokes and confused images. Maybe it was pretty much the same for Gil, though he had an older brother with a wild reputation.

In any case, Gil asked if I could get myself home. I said yes and, after a hesitation, he turned and left running, his black tennis shoes scuttling through the leaves.

I sat up and checked myself. My underpants were stretched out of shape but intact, my blouse in place, my skin soiled, and a dampness down there that had surely come from him. Chinquapin kernels hard as pebbles had punctured my bottom. All of that effort and he had actually done nothing to really scar me. Either he hadn't the heart or the ability to do it, that's what I would later surmise, though, of course, I'd never know.

On the way back, I stopped in a small clearing, breathing slowly and trying to catch up with myself. A big patch of clover growing tiny blue flowers stretched back into the shadows. And there were yellow bees, honey bees, flitting in and out of the clover and sailing past me on the way to their hive, the Queen, I'm sure. All around a silence, the kind of reverent quiet that you can find in the deep woods along with a silver-gray sky above the green and slight breeze in the treetops, speaking to you. I felt grateful, as if this place had been offered to keep me sane and make up for the pain that was now mostly inside of me, in my heart and mind. Never have I been so thankful that I was free and alone.

I went on home, crept through the house straight into the bathroom and, using sudsy water, washed myself with hands raw from sliding down the vine. Through the bathroom door, my mother called out in her alarm voice—"where have you been?"

"Outside," I said, "I started feeling bad. I have a headache."

"You never have headaches. Come out here and let me see," she said. She checked for fever, told me to take an aspirin and lie down before supper, saying nothing more about being late, which is what I knew would happen.

My mother was predictable, my dad predictable, my older sister, married with a baby on the way, less so. She easily flew off the handle but was often full of enough warmth to make up for it. My younger brother was as predictable as any eight-year-old boy could be, I guess. I always thought that being the middle one among three is probably the easiest, especially if the youngest is a boy.

This was a Thursday. Friday morning, Gil wasn't on the bus. He wasn't at school.

Saturday it turned sunny and cold, at least cold enough for a jacket and warm socks. In the morning, I did homework, talked on the phone, and then helped Mother in the kitchen putting up field peas, which my father and little brother had shelled out on the back porch. Afterward, I took my brother on a long walk to the store near town for baking soda to bake the Sunday bread and two cones, probably orange sherbet for him, lemon for me.

The next morning before church, out in front of the sanctuary, I learned of the accident from a boy in my class. At first, I didn't believe him. I asked him again, "Gil McDaniel?" And he was certain, "yes, it was Gil alright." He had found out last night. I was suddenly sick, dazed, like the earth under my feet was rocking back and forth. Without making a great effort to hold onto myself, I would have surely thrown up. Before the boy could say anything else, I backed off and looked for Mother and found her standing with a circle of friends near the church steps. Dad's arm was around her shoulder, which told me it was true.

I went over there slowly. I stopped outside the circle, trying to make sense of their empty faces and listening to what was being said about Gil. Gil McDaniel was now the center of their attention, as if his death had suddenly made him worthwhile for gossip, when for all his life, I'm sure they'd never given him a second thought. He wasn't a church member; his family didn't go to our church. At one point, after a man in a felt hat, Brother Vernon, had said a piece about God's will, the minister's wife, Sister Rozelle, a tall woman with an abundance of blond-red hair piled on her head, spoke up. "Well, whatever happens, God's finger stirs everything," her voice firm and jarring. She was a powerful presence in not only the church but the community as well.

I found myself leaning against my mother, shaking. She hugged me. "Oh, Honey, I'm so sorry," she said. "I know he was a friend of yours."

Little by little, I picked up the story. Despite the unseasonably cold weather, a group of boys had gone down to the river at a place called the Big Eddy, a mile or so outside of town. They planned to camp and fish but then, despite the cold, decided to swim on a dare. For some reason or maybe no reason at all except that he was good at it, Gil climbed a tall tree and jumped out of it, diving into the water. He never came up. Late that evening, his body was found in a patch of cattails at the confluence of the river and Angelina Creek.

When I had heard all that I could stand to hear, I backed away, circled a line of low hedges, and hurried down a pathway that went around behind the church. There were parked cars back there and beyond them a grove of persimmon trees. Persimmons were scattered over the ground, most of them red and rotting, others half green. My legs began to quiver and, despite the rotten persimmons, I sat down in my light blue skirt on the cold earth.

For a little while, I managed my black feelings—despair. But eventually the words from Sister Rozelle came to haunt me. I pictured a finger pointing down from on high. Had God put Gil and me together and then stirred us up to see how we'd react? An unavoidable thing to want to know. Soon, the thought emerged that if I hadn't been so quick to run with him into the woods, so excited about climbing the tree, he would never have thought to come at me. Or if I hadn't worn a skirt that day or not teased him about his grammar, when it was no worse than a lot of kids. Or if I had slapped him good and hard when he first tried to kiss me. Why did he think I'd want to kiss him anyway?

I began to feel cold tears dragging down my cheeks, as if my eyes had become fountains fed by bad water. He drowned, trying to breathe that cold, silty river water. It must've been a painful way to die, I thought, and then kept on thinking, while all those grow-ups in front of the church were drawing their own conclusions about a young death. Though just fourteen, I knew better than they did and cursed their words. He wasn't careless or marked for death, just a scrappy boy who got excited climbing trees, whether unusual trees that hid out in the deep woods or ordinary ones that chose to grow beside a river.

Edith's Goats

There is going to be a wedding at the old Bethel Church, which to Edith's mind seems peculiar. As far as she knows, nothing happens there these days except local club meetings and funerals for families with plots in the church's ancient cemetery. Then comes a jolt, the bride's family name—Cantwell.

Holding onto herself, Edith spreads the paper, *The Sour Springs Record*, across her kitchen table so a strip of sunlight from a far window falls over a picture of the bride standing beside a horse. A tall, handsome girl with a self-assured smile and dark hair that disappears behind her shoulders. Raised in Houston, the article says, her father in investments, her mother an artist and gallery owner. A grandfather, Eldon Cantwell, grew up in the Sour Springs community. No mention of the man's wife, but there is timberland and oil holdings and an old family estate on a lake in the thickets not far from Woodville. Among the bride's passions is historical preservation, thus her choice of the little church, which her ancestors had helped build "working as a community the way they did in those days."

Adjusting her glasses, Edith tries to finish the article, even as her mind clings to the name back up there, Eldon Cantwell—which has to be the Eldon Cantwell of fifty-some-odd years ago, and her heated imagination depicts a lean, long-jawed, dark-haired, arrogant boy on a horse. All at once, her breath gives out and she sits back, shoves the paper aside, and then in a rush of emotions, pushes it across the table onto the floor.

Breakfast done, Edith heaves herself up and begins to clear the table but hasn't the will for it right then. She takes a bottle of Coca-Cola from the refrigerator and, in her bedroom, cigarettes and a book of matches from a drawer in the bedside table.

It is the first week of June, warm, crystal sparks of dew in the yard grass. In her loose work trousers and old blue shirt, she sits on the front porch and smokes a stale Winston, drinking the coke from an iced tea glass, concentrating on her Boer goats, twenty-seven of them now, beyond the rail fence in a pasture that slopes down two hundred yards or so to the country road out in front of the house. Two years ago, after Harlan died, she cleared the place of farm animals, went through a period of depressed boredom, and finally accepted a young neighbor's offer to go into the goat business with him. It's one of those health things, a lot better for you than beef, Max Kembro said, excited about the prospects. He swore that, in a few years, everybody in the cities were going to be eating goat cheese and goat meat. The ranch and farm magazines and a man he knew at the state Extension Service were practically guaranteeing it.

Edith put up half the money and the pasture. Max and his teenage son took on most of the work. In time, she was pleased with the way the goats kept the weeds and briers down and, also, she came to realize, offered company. Goats were clean, cheaper than cattle to raise, and liked people, at least they liked to see her coming and would rush to nuzzle her when she let them. In their voices—*bleating*, people mistakenly called it—she detected a human sound, especially from the youngsters. Sometimes at night if they are riled by something, she lies in bed and listens to the kids and grown-ups jabbering at one another, gossiping and entertaining themselves, she likes to think, perhaps calling out and wondering about her.

In a little while, Edith stubs out the half-smoked cigarette and goes through the fence gate into the pasture and walks out among them, spreading vitamin-laced feed from a burlap sack kept in a little shed out there. The babies curl in behind their mothers and some of the nannies come up to her, shoving, baring denture-looking teeth stained green from weeds and clover, asking to nibble from her hand. Sometimes she will grip a pair of spiked horns and wrestle for a minute with one of the young ones who especially like jostling with her.

Edith empties the bag, flapping the last of the grain from it, ties her gray hair back, and then in a fit of distraction and sheer willfulness, undoes the top buttons of her shirt and slips it off her plump shoulders to let the sun work on her freckled skin. As a girl, she had shot up before others her age, a beanpole by the time she was twelve or thirteen, and then with little warning, her figure took shape, breasts appeared before other girls', which was an embarrassment. The junior high boys seemed indifferent, but over in the high school next door, they noticed and she would feel the heat of their eyes at times. For a while, it confused and distracted her. At the beginning of spring that year, there was a school play where she and another girl danced and sang a song that was popular then, "Blue Skies." And while they were performing in short blue satin dresses and knit stockings, boys began to whistle. Eldon Cantwell, who everybody knew, was one of them. Sitting near the front of the auditorium with the high school seniors, you couldn't miss him.

In any case, later there was a certain afternoon when she was walking along the road in front of the high school toward town and heard a horse coming up behind her, the hooves clopping and then a leather saddle creaking. "Hey. Hey, girl" was how he started out and then asked if she wouldn't like to climb up. "I'll trot her for you" are words she would remember. Probably she didn't answer, but his voice sent a shiver through her, an excitement, even as she dropped her head and hurried on.

The next time was different. She was with some other girls and, out of something, a faked brazenness or disappointment with herself over the last time, she didn't refuse. Eldon Cantwell leaned out of the saddle, grasped an arm, and lifted her up behind him like she weighed no more than a sack of feathers. There were laughs and teasing from her friends. They galloped a quarter of a mile to where the road circled a big hickory on the edge of downtown and then trotted back, ending up behind the high school in a growth of trees where the boys who rode horses to school tied them up. She slid down. "Once you've grow up, we'll do it again," Eldon Cantwell called after her, showing off for the popular crowd, boys and girls, too, who were gathered there.

His strength is what had finally stuck with her—and the jerky, unpredictable way he used the reins, which seemed to confuse the horse as well as force her to lean against him and grasp his waist to keep her balance. It was a big horse, a long way to the ground.

Once the nannies and kids are fed and she has filled the water trough, Edith goes around the house and on to the back pasture where Max has isolated the two billys, an old one and a young buck. They both can get ornery, especially to the little ones that stick close to their mothers. If you didn't watch, they will move in and try to keep the kids from sucking and also butt and pester them when they try to graze. Max has decided that he will have to make a wether of the old one to quiet him down and then start fattening him up for the packing house. He is stout, this old buck, and still strong, with a long back, horns that curve to a wicket point, and a beard as ragged as an old hermit's.

When Edith enters the pen with the feed buckets, the two bucks, standing at a distance from each other, pep up. She sets the buckets far apart so there will be no fighting over who gets what. Then as she starts to work spreading hay, she hears a car coming up the gravel drive. It stops in front of the house. *Oh god*, she tells herself, *last thing I want's company*. But then it's Willa Starnes, no surprise. In a minute, she comes striding across the backyard in a flowered skirt, waving her sunhat. And a thought flashes in Edith's conscience that over coffee, which is surely what Willa has come for, she will spread out the newspaper and bit by bit find a way to confide in her and, perhaps, in the telling of it release some of the poison that has been circulating in her blood, infecting her soul all morning. Since Harlan died, Willa has become a frequent caller, one of the few women left that Edith cares to be around anymore.

"I caught you playing with the goats again," Willa calls out, still moving toward her. "I thought you were the boss and Max was supposed to do all the work."

"Well, I get bored," Edith says. "I wouldn't call this real work anyway."

"I brought sweet corn muffins," Willa says. She has them on a covered plate.

Willa is something like seven years younger, sixty-one, though still girlish most of the time, her hair cut fashionably with red highlights and her person on the plump side, but that plump that strikes you as warm and inviting. She admires herself a little too much, Edith thinks, but who ever had a friend they couldn't complain about.

"You want to hear something I ought not to say," she told Edith a month or so after Harlan's funeral. "I'm envious, flat jealous of you living on your own. No one to have to tend to. You know what I want more than anything else? To be single for a day or two and have a date. Go out with a man I hardly know and hear him say something I didn't expect him to say."

In the kitchen, Edith clears the table of the breakfast things and puts coffee on and retrieves the newspaper from the trash can under the sink where she had finally stuffed it. It is wrinkled, damp with food stains.

"You got a cigarette?" Willa asks, twitching her fingers. According to Willa, she doesn't smoke but when they are together. Edith brings the pack from the bedroom. She strikes a match for Willa's cigarette and then uses the flame to light one for herself. She sets out an ash tray and the corn muffins and pours coffee and lays the filthy paper neatly folded on a corner of the table.

"I have lost fourteen pounds almost," Willa exclaims, without glancing at the paper. "Does it show?"

"You look good."

"Actually, my life's falling apart," she blurts, wrinkles appearing around her mouth.

"Now, Willa."

"I mean it. Dear God, it's true. I know I shouldn't be burdening you," she goes on, "but I'm having an affair with a man. Not an old man, either." She exhales smoke, coughing a cough that turns to a feeble laugh that sputters out. Her cheeks bunch up and eyes glisten.

Before Edith can think to open her mouth, Willa starts in. He is a man from Port Arthur and they met at the Valero gas station on the outskirts of town, standing by their cars. "I was on one side of the pump, pumping," Willa says. "He was on the other. We exchanged some words." An hour later, he came to her table at the Burl's Cafe.

"He sat down," Willa says, nervously tapping the cigarette against her coffee saucer. "And that's where it started. He's not completely handsome, a little overweight, but my god, gentle, and he talks about things I never talk about and listens to me and has the nicest fingernails. All my life, I've been wanting to sit down to supper with a man with clean fingernails."

She won't touch a muffin but reaches out for Edith's hand and sniffles and opens her mouth again and doesn't close it for the next half hour.

In the pasture under a blue sky hung with sheer white clouds, Edith leads the nannie who they called Freya up onto the milking platform and coaxes her head into the stanchion and clamps the bar shut over her neck. Max or his son, Max Junior, who they call M.J., usually do the milking, but this evening they went straight to the back pasture with the equipment to make a wether of the old billy and Edith offered to milk. With cows, milking can be a chore, but she doesn't mind the nannies. Give them something to munch on and they relax and chew their cuds and you can hear their teeth clicking as milk shoots easily into the pail. And they enjoy conversation, a little soothing talk or a nice song settles them into a near reverie.

Which is a comfort after killing half the morning with Willa. Once Willa left, the wrinkled newspaper had traveled from the breakfast table to a far corner of the kitchen counter and, finally, the top of the refrigerator. Now, squeezing milk from Freya, speaking gently to her, the picture of the bride sweeps into Edith's mind and she thinks of the Bethel church. An old relic kept up all these years by the community—its deep green lawn, cherry laurel lining the walkways, and the original brass bell in a little steeple on the roof peak because, at one time, the building was both a church and two-room schoolhouse. It's there she and her older brother attended first and second grade until the bus started running into Sour Springs.

She can't deny she was taken with Eldon Cantwell. The thrill and pleasant redolence of the horse and the sensation of her hands on the boy's sharp ribs had remained and she looked for every chance to be noticed again. He would appear across the school yard full of energy, trading friendly punches with boys, flirting with girls, smoothing his hair back over his head, about the most popular boy there.

It took nearly a month, Easter time. She had stayed late to help decorate the hallways and auditorium, so she missed the bus home and started into town to try to catch a ride with somebody going out her way. Walking past the high school, the tall, narrow windows glazed by sunlight, there was a stroke of luck. There was Eldon Cantwell back under the trees. He was saddling up, the sorrel horse throwing its head. Edith brought her books up close to her face, imagining how to close the distance between them without looking eager and silly, what to say if he noticed her. Then, a boy appeared from the back door of the school. He was running hard with his head down toward Eldon Cantwell. She knew him, that boy, not his name, but who he was. His mother worked in the cafeteria, ladling out food, checking as you washed your tray after eating and often, in the afternoon, she cleaned the girls' restroom in Edith's building. Her son was about a third grader with a rough haircut and, as he ran, a cotton shirt that bellowed up on his back.

From a distance, she watched Eldon Cantwell smooth the boy's yellow hair with a hand and then a comb from his back pocket. He lifted the boy into the saddle, swung up behind him, and they started off under the trees on into the woods. Edith caught her breath and, gathering courage, set out after them across the ball field toward the spot where they had disappeared. It was simple; she would move softly, looking for a way to intercept them and, at some point, appear, pretending she had just happened along, a brave girl at ease in the woods. It would impress Eldon Cantwell, she imagined. He would invite her up onto the horse as before and they would ride beneath the trees, the three of them scrunched together, and then eventually they would come out of the shadows and ride on into the heart of town, the start of something.

The thing was they quickly vanished into the bush. She hurried. There was a path, but she skirted it and moved on into the thickets and through the trees, using her books to push at choked undergrowth when it rose up to block the way. Feeble sunlight fluttered down through the trees. There was an armadillo's ravaged shell, a squirrel on the move overhead, and an unnerving silence. Edith got lost. She waited briefly, listening, and then went on and a minute later heard the horse snort once again and followed the sound. At last, through the foliage, she spotted the horse and nearby there was Eldon Cantwell and the boy in a small clearing in the soft shadow of a gum tree.

Nervous as to what to do, Edith moved on through the undergrowth as close as her courage would take her. Lifting her skirt, she went to her knees, set her books aside, and inched over leaf mold into a tangle of leafy vines. What she witnessed from there was more like fleeting images than reality. The boy was on the ground shirtless and Eldon Cantwell was stripping him of his jeans. Then, Eldon Cantwell's boots came off and, in a moment, his own trousers as well. She would remember the boy's thin chicken bone arms and chicken-white skin and Eldon Cantwell's bare legs and muted voice drifting in the utter quiet of the woods. She was confused by what her eyes were trying to tell her and stiff as a stick, while at the same time trembling all over. It went on and the boy knew what was expected of him and he played that role without emotion—what Edith would never have words for. She couldn't continue watching and couldn't move nor turn her head away. To silence a scream, she bit into her fist and sunk deeper into the damp leaves until, at last, she couldn't breathe or didn't want to breathe, a condition that would revisit her imagination from time to time for years to come.

After freeing Freya from the stanchion, Edith milks five more nannies, enough to fill three pails. She carries the milk to the house and places it in the refrigerator for Max to pick up, all but the little that she keeps back for coffee. While at the kitchen sink making lemonade, she hears Max and M.J. on the front porch.

"We're too filthy to come in the house," Max says, accepting the cold glasses Edith has for them. There is dried blood on Max's hands and the billed cap that's pushed back on his head. Drops are sprinkled in a pattern on the boy's face. Edith comes back with a warm cloth and, holding M.J. by the chin, scrubs his cheeks and forehead.

"He was kicking," M.J. tells, eyes squeezed shut as she works on him.

"Don't give me any details," Edith tells him, meaning it.

Max is lean, work-muscled, caring, as good a man as she has ever known. He and her own son had been friends all their lives. Once, she had sort of hoped that her daughter would take up with Max, but Denise had ambitions that didn't include country life. She married on a beach near Corpus Christi and was soon divorced and moved into a new existence down there that Edith sometimes envied. Edith's son ended up over in Louisiana, Baton Rouge, working in city government.

As Max is leaving, he asks her to go out in an hour or two and get the old billy up and get him walking and to be sure he's taking water. "He'll be a little testy," he warns her.

At last, she's alone. As nearly always, she has supper alone at the dining table, fresh greens and a stew with pork simmering in it. Edith won't touch goat meat, has never taken a bite of it, though Max keeps offering, swears it's delicious, especially hickory barbequed. There is no logical excuse she can give him or herself. She and Harlan slaughtered cattle and hogs and squirrels and deer and about every other wild creature, but now, maybe it is her tender old age, she won't raise her own hand, much less a knife against one of the goats. When Max sells one or takes a few to the packing house, she stays out of sight.

She goes to bed early, reads a little, and wakes at three and again at four, audibly grinding her teeth. The dentist made a plastic guard for them, but she has never gotten used to the thing, afraid she might choke on it in her sleep. At seven, Max comes to check on the billy and Janine, his wife, in her tight jeans and hippy sandals, goes into the pasture to do the milking. The morning is bright, the air drier than usual, an orange-tinted sky.

"That old buck will be happier now he doesn't have females on the brain," Janine says to Edith as they walk up to the pen where Max is bathing the goat's wound with disinfectant. Janine yells out to the ruined buck, "Just wallow in your leisure, hear. You'll get plenty of apple cores to grow nice and fat on."

They are leaning on the top rail of the pen drinking coffee Janine brought in a thermos, the expensive kind of coffee you grind at home, which is, in fact, a little burnt tasting to Edith's mind. Max found his wife at a community college in the suburbs of Houston, a city girl who had quickly taken to country life.

"Come over and we'll take the canoe to the river," she says, clutching Edith's arm. "I know where there's a ton of berries along the bank."

"I can't." Edith pauses to catch up her breath. "I'm going to the beauty shop in a little while and this afternoon to a wedding."

That decision was made sometime in the early morning as the light of dawn forced the shadows from the corners of her bedroom. It is not what she wants to do. It scares her to think about it. But the opportunity has presented itself and she is obliged by a power outside herself demanding that it has to be done. If nothing else, an obligation to judge how the years had scarred him, how bitter and useless his life might be.

In the beginning, back then, she had been too stunned, defeated, to deal with all that she had witnessed and do what ought to have been done. Ugly pictures were stamped in her head but with no words fit to tell even her best friend, much less her mother or the boy's mother or anyone of authority who might do something about it. The anguish, a kind of self-condemnation, stirred a fire of shame. And so she went about the school in an altered state, hiding her face when the yellow-haired boy—he was called Buster, she learned—appeared or she glimpsed Eldon Cantwell going about his business, untroubled.

Then, she saw them together once more, maybe a week or so later, the flow of time had escaped her. The boy was brushing Eldon Cantwell's big sorrel horse, a soda pop in one hand. There were other high school boys there with him under the trees. Edith rushed away but was later drawn back to the grounds of the high school to check once more and, this time, Eldon Cantwell and the boy were gone. A saddle lay under the trees, so they must have ridden out bareback.

Her first thought was of the boy's mother but then she found herself heading for the grade school building, almost running, as if the structure might vanish before she got there. She went through a side door, down the dim hallway with its familiar scent of floor wax and unclean little bodies, past the open doors of empty classrooms. Lingering in the hallway, she imagined herself entering Mrs. Pernell's room, her former fourth grade teacher, the one she most trusted. She saw herself sit down before her desk and explain in clear, powerful words what she had witnessed and Mrs. Pernell's sudden alarm and then Mr. Gantt, the principal, and others rushing into the woods to get their hands on Eldon Cantwell.

That's what her mind conjured up but not what happened. Mrs. Pernell was there all right, working at her desk. But at the doorway, Edith's throat clogged like there was a pit caught in it, her courage shook, and she backed away. Then came the forethought that even if they happened to believe what she said about Eldon Cantwell, she might, in fact, be the one accused: *You lay there watching that? Why were you in the woods with a high school senior anyway? You've been keeping this secret how long?"*

Thank God above he graduated in May, went off to a college people said, and she never saw him again. Buster she was forced to see on occasion all through her years in high school; from afar, she watched him taking on the features of youth and wondered at the dark thoughts and feelings that might affect his growing up—and his mother, a small, tight-lipped woman in a hairnet, she encountered practically every day.

It changed her, those few minutes in the woods, or at least that's what she came to believe. At worst, it seemed that she had played a part in it and, at rare times, the years of her young life were shrunk down to that one day. She never spoke a word to anyone. In high school, there were joys, she was popular by all accounts, had a boyfriend for a while, but was always careful and avoided sex. At the same time, she developed a hatred of the memory of Eldon Cantwell and a hope that in the natural scheme of things or by God's hand, if that's what it took, he would be punished.

A year after graduating, about the time she was thinking of going off on her own, maybe to college in San Antonio where she had a girlfriend, she met Harlan Raines, who was nine years older, a grown man who had moved back home to take over his family's butane business. She fell in love with him, a growing, attentive sort of love, the place they finally bought, the two good children they raised, and was truly never sorry about any of it.

Edith wears a pale floral dress with a small jacket and new low-heeled shoes, her hair in a bun at the nape of her neck. She carries white cotton gloves in her fist. It is four miles along country roads to the church. At first, she drives on past, observing the crowd out in front of the place, and then a mile up the road forces herself to turn around. She parks along with other cars on the roadside, her car pointed toward home, gathers herself, and makes her way up the freshly cut embankment to the lawn and into the crowd. There are more dressed-up people and agitated kids and frilly dresses than surely the little church can hold. All are strangers, prosperous city people, it seems, and chatty, their voices drifting in the air. She approaches a man standing a little apart, smoking.

"Are you bride or groom?" she asks him, keeping up appearances.

He glances up and coughs into his fist and says "groom, I suppose," though it was his wife who has dragged him here. He has a hesitant voice and splotched, red face, an alcoholic's face, which makes Edith, in her nervousness, want to reach out and take his arm, but instead, she chats, telling him about the old church building, that she had gone to school here. She points out the bell on the rooftop that rang for class to start. After a few minutes, she asks if he happens to know of the bride's grandfather, "Eldon Cantwell it would be."

"Mr. Cantwell? Over that way." The man raises his cigarette, pointing. "The tall one with grey hair in that group."

The man's back is turned. Edith makes her way around huddled groups toward him. She sees a tall, old man in a blue suit, thin, with sloped shoulders, and an abundance of fleecy white hair. A shock: he is deeply aged but still, in her mind, recognizable. At an angle, she studies his face, the long jaw, sharp bones beneath his eyes, surely an important man who might have once been in politics or overseen an estate. As a young man beside him speaks, this Eldon Cantwell lays a hand on his shoulder as if steadying himself. An eight or nine-year-old girl appears and grabs the old man's hand, smiling up at him. A woman also comes forward, middle-aged, in an electric wheelchair. She is gaunt in what seems an expensive silk dress, sparse brown hair, barely able to hold her head up. Stiffly, Eldon Cantwell leans down to kiss her cheek. Edith watches, tense and angry at what he seems to be, realizing that she has come with expectations of something less.

From inside the church, soft music rises and people begin to fall into place to go in. Edith glances around at confident faces and bright jewelry, the women's hats, a scent of perfume that brings pictures of gardenias into her head. The music, something classical that seems familiar, comes from two young women, one playing a flute, the other a guitar. Ushers, young boys wearing cloth gloves, coax her into a pew near the back and she finds herself at the very end between a grim-faced woman with heavy shoulders and a huge arrangement of delphiniums. The little church is overrun with them, delphiniums, calla lilies, and other white and blue flowers carefully placed.

Edith pulls on her gloves and allows her eyes to close, absorbing the music. As it dies away, she finds she wants to pee, which makes her smile for a moment and then settle back to endure it. When the wedding march starts, she grasps the pew in front of her and stands with the others, recalling those two years of school here, how the room had been arranged, two students to a desk, a young teacher named Miss Devaney she could not quite visualize except that she had bobbed hair, which made her seem worldly.

The minister wears a black robe and scarlet stole, the groom beside him a little stout but handsome enough. They come together, the enviable couple, and say their vows. Stout boy and slim girl so made up she is barely recognized as the one in the newspaper. At the end, there is a long kiss. Recorded music rises again. The bride lifts her dress and they come down from the platform to pause where her father and mother and Eldon Cantwell are waiting. The whole thing an intimate spectacle, a bright jewel of a wedding. It doesn't matter Edith tells herself but, of course, it does.

Outside, feathered clouds and bright sunlight bless the gathering crowd. The bride and groom come hurrying through a shower of rice to a chauffeured car and the big, black Buick pulls away down the long drive out onto the country road heading god knows where. Edith watches all this and then, somewhat numb like after a long church service, backs away to circle the crowd, thinking it is over now, that's that. She wants to go home, feels the need of it in her limbs and starts for the car down a clay path lined with laurel hedges where the man she spoke to earlier stands alone, fidgeting as he lights a cigarette. The sight of him slouched over, complicit in his own destruction, provokes her, spilling a wave of pent-up anger.

Drawing herself up, Edith turns around and makes her way back into the crowd, then on to a circle of men, five or six of them, where stands Eldon Cantwell. Unnoticed, and without waiting to be noticed, Edith steps forward and breaks into the conversation, trembling a little.

"I believe I knew you," she says at Cantwell, the strain in her voice unfamiliar to her own ears. The small circle opens up. The man raises his eyes, which are drawn and damply red.

Edith says, "I knew you in high school, Sour Springs High School, a long time ago."

"Oh...?" The voice is phlegmy, muttered.

"It's true," Edith goes on. "You took me on your horse once. And we had a friend in common, a young boy, a lot younger than we were...in grade school. You might remember his mother, she worked in the cafeteria there. His name was Buster. Buster. You were friendly with him, I happen to know that."

The old man studies her, wipes his mouth. "What do you mean?"

"He was a good boy." Edith's breath cuts the words off. She stops to breathe. "Eight years old," she speaks into his face. "Don't say you don't remember him."

"Lady, I never saw you in my life." Eldon Cantwell glances around at the others. "Anybody know her?"

"You've seen me all right. You abused that child!"

And then barely aware of herself, she tears a glove off, steps forward, and strikes him, a flashing, open-handed blow across the jaw, stinging her own hand. Cantwell stumbles back and, at once, someone grabs her. Others join in. She jerks and squirms, slapping at whoever she can reach. She wrenches free. "Don't touch me!" she lets out. There is a brief standoff. Edith alone, daring them. With eyes burning, she scans their faces, turns at once and, grasping the glove, starts out across the grass, walking fast and then running, loping in those damn new shoes.

She drives home at a speed far faster than she should on the narrow country road, feverish. Feverish still when she reaches the house, when sitting in a slip before her dresser mirror, scrubbing makeup from her face with tissue and cold cream, revealing familiar fissures and soft wrinkles, wondering at this woman before her with ash-grey hair and blue-green eyes that seem more steady than usual and then little by little, comes a free breath. It wasn't enough, just the act of a child, but it brings an unexpected smile, something that she can live with.

At some point, the phone rings and as Edith lets it ring, she feels all those other eyes on her, bewildered men in white collars and ties. They will remember her, the power she wielded, and this Eldon Cantwell, nursing an abused cheek, will remember her, too. Maybe not from back then, but from this moment on. She wonders if he can even recall the boy. Have there been others?

When the phone rings again sometime later, it is Max asking her to go out to the pen and check on the old billy. "He ought to be up and getting around," he says. "There shouldn't be any bleeding." It is twilight when she finally goes out there in her pajamas, barefoot on the prickly grass and new thistles. The air is damp and fresh, shades of pink dying above the woods. On seeing her, the old billy hefts himself onto his four legs and stands stark still in his corner, taking her in. She places her hands on the top rail of the pen and, with a touch of pity, watches him in his misery. He is stumbling some and as the young buck rises up across the pen, starts to bawl.

Bible Music

I was thirty-five then, pretty much settled in mind and spirit and closer to being in love than I had ever been in my life. Then, we met at a cabin she had in the mountains outside of Wolf Creek and after a week there, snowed in much of the time, breathing each other's air and eating each other's cooking, it all fell apart. One morning, after a last surly night, I got up before dawn, stacked armloads of kindling and firewood on the front porch, and packed my car, an old Mercedes 250 that wasn't made for mountain driving. Getting down to the main road through the pines wasn't bad, but before long, it started to snow again and half an hour later it was so heavy the wipers could hardly handle it. I got behind a big truck that was straining to make the grade and, creeping along, trying to forget myself by listening to the Kronos Quartet's new jazz album, my phone rang.

It wasn't her, which surprised me. It was my dad, which surprised me even more. Whenever we talked, it was me calling him. I turned the music down so the strings were just a whisper.

"Where are you?" he said, which was how he started out once I got the mobile phone. And I told him and then told him about the blowing snow and icy road and the big truck up ahead and that driving with one hand I was putting my life at risk.

"Your mother's gone to North Carolina," he said, ignoring everything else. It was crazy he would say it like that, with a dramatic tick in his voice because the truth was they had been living apart for three years now.

"She came and got the rest of her stuff," Dad went on. "I don't know why North Carolina, if she's met somebody or what. Anyway," he said, "I've got a favor to ask. Look, I need you to come down here." And he said it again and then assured me he was serious and when I said there wasn't anything I could do about it, he said it's not about Lois. "It's something else entirely."

"Okay, what else."

"Not something to talk about on the phone," he said. We went back and forth and when I saw he wasn't about to let up, I convinced him I'd call back as soon as it was safe.

Once I got over the mountain, the weather suddenly changed, like it can at those altitudes. There was no more snow and the sun came out, lighting the pines, and the road went down into a valley and I crossed a stream into a small settlement that included a restaurant and gas pumps. After filling the car, I went inside and ordered breakfast from the nice woman behind the counter, a large woman in baggy pants and a man's flannel shirt, sixty or more, I'd guess. She had an appealing laugh, a round, wind-chapped face and wooly white hair showing some of her scalp. *Cancer, chemo* are the words that came to mind and I wanted to ask her and hear her say that whatever it was was gone and she was doing well. Instead, we talked about her rhubarbs and fallow garden and then the condition of the roads. And all the while, in my mind, was the restless sound of Dad's voice. I purchased a book of highway maps from a display and, studying it together, the woman and I decided on the route I should take to reach a road that would start me on the way to Louisiana.

There was no mobile signal down in this valley, so I called Dad on the payphone. It was a short conversation that began with him refusing again to say why he had to see me and ended with him saying he didn't want to hold me up any longer.

Outside, I used a hose to clean mud and ice from under the fenders and then wiped down the old Mercedes with a damp cloth so it would feel cared for, my conscience reminding me that Mom and Dad had done everything for me and never asked for anything substantial in return. I owed him and thinking of making a down payment was good for my spirits. In any case, I had some time to kill before I had to be back in Las Vegas. I started out for Raton Pass. Before long, I had Ali Farka and Ry Cooder's *Talking Timbuktu* in the tape deck and, with their absolution, decided that not only was I doing right by Dad, but also, driving home to Louisiana in the middle of winter was the perfect way to get her out of my life.

Late in the afternoon, I crossed the Texas border into the Panhandle. The flat landscape and scrub trees and cactus were covered in a warm blanket of snow to the horizon, all that space, all that silence. I stayed awake on coffee from a thermos I'd purchased at a truck stop while listening to some music that I hadn't played in a long time, including a film score by Shostakovich about a romantic Russian couple wandering in the snow to escape from a war, a piece I'd brought along for us to listen to.

Music became part of my life early on. My mother's fault. She raised my older sister and me on music the way the kids we went to school with in Lafayette were raised on the church. To hear her tell it, she didn't start playing the piano until she was in high school and a teacher there convinced her she had talent and in time, Mom said, playing the piano was as natural as picking flowers. Her family was poor, so when she got a partial scholarship to a small college in New Orleans, she made ends meet by playing wherever she could, mostly on the street for the tourists, not the piano, but the electric violin. That's where she met Dad, on the street. He was with a survey crew, had a steady salary. They moved in together and he paid for her schooling, at least a part of it, and, somewhere along the way, they got married. After graduating, Mom began teaching music in the high schools in and around Lafayette and Dad got on with a government survey operation that did a lot of work in the swamps and thickets and along the coast in Louisiana and all over the south.

Adele came along and then me. Mom started us out on the piano before we could ride a bicycle. All music comes from the piano, she would say, and only when she was satisfied did she let me take up the violin and Adele the cello, and we both played guitar and, with Mom's coaxing, Dad got to where he could strum cords on the mandolin. Weekends they would get half drunk and our house was full of music and friends and during those times, except for their occasional cussing fights, it seemed everything was just the way it was supposed to be.

After high school, Adele went off to college in San Antonio, met a young Hispanic man there, and moved to El Paso where he went to work with the Border Patrol. I went to a college in Seattle studying music, mostly paid for by Mom and Dad, a life changing experience. After graduation, I hoped to get with an orchestra but soon realized that, for me, there was no future in classical music and so, trying to suspend the next chapter in my life, I spent several years playing in different small bands all over the Northwest and in Canada. I met an old sax player who told me that, if I came to Las Vegas, he would help me get work. And before I was hardly settled in, I got on with a show band and stayed with it until I couldn't abide the low pay and brutal hours anymore. Quit it and got with a manager and slowly carved out a living, and then a career playing violin whenever I could, fiddling when I had to, piano when no one else was available. Casinos, bars, conventions, studio work, big parties—it's all in Las Vegas and has been good to me.

I drove until past midnight and stopped at a motel outside of Athens, Texas. Slept ten hours and drove down through eastern Texas on a series of highways which run through a part of the country my dad grew up in, "poor enough to know that hunger gave you a hell of a stomachache," he would tell us when in the mood to teach us something. Dad had no compunctions about opening up to Adele and me. Or anyone else with ears. I wonder if he ever had a thought in his head he didn't express to somebody, often more than once, which is another thing that drove my mother crazy.

His father was a farmer and part-time preacher. A hard man with a predictable temper is the way my dad described him. He baptized his second wife, Dad's mother, and every one of his offspring, including Dad, in the same water off a sandbar in a stream in the low country of East Texas called Village Creek. Dad and his two brothers and sister spent their evenings memorizing and arguing Bible passages among each other and the Preacher and sometimes other kids whose parents sent them to the house to get their Bible education. That's the way I learned to picture it. And recalling it, turning it over in my head, helped to explain what Dad was going to tell me when we got together.

∾

Late in the afternoon, I turned off the black tar road and crossed the short wooden bridge that spanned a drainage ditch in front of Dad's house, a place he and Mom had bought when they moved from town several years ago. It was a pleasant, sturdy house raised a few feet off the earth against the rains and high water with a steep roof of cypress shingles set among thickets and water tupelos, a half-hour's drive outside of Lafayette.

Dad was off the front porch and out to the car before I could get the door open. "I was expecting you this morning," he said.

"I had to take time to sleep," I told him. He threw his arms around me and held on for a long minute.

"She's in Asheville," he said, then stepped back and looked me over.

"I know, I talk to her," I said. "She likes it there. It's beautiful country."

"Still driving this old Mercedes-Benz," he said, and slapped the roof.

"Not old, vintage."

There was something wildly different about him: his beard was gone. He had had a rusty-red beard and mustache for years. Now, the lower part of his face and his lean jawline was bare and pale below sunbaked cheeks and narrow eyes, red-rimmed eyes.

He went to the trunk for my bag. I stood and stretched and looked around at the big trees circling his plot of land. The yard looked newly trimmed. Holly shrubs grew along a gravel walkway and wax myrtles stood at the corners of the house. There were loquat trees and pecans.

I asked about the dog.

"Belle? I had to bury her. She's back behind the house. There's a marker," he said.

"I'm sorry to hear that." And I was. Belle was a beautiful little girl, a water dog with brown and yellow spots they'd raised from a pup.

There was a stew on the stove and the house was filled with the scent of cayenne pepper and garlic. When Dad was away on a job, sometimes a week or more at a time, Adele and I prayed for him to hurry up and get home so he could take a turn in the kitchen. Though there was Cajun blood in Mother's family, she had no patience for cooking. You could hear her cussing the pots and pans and taste her anguish in the clumped-up rice and canned vegetables and other stuff that ended up on our plates and in our stomachs.

Once Dad and I had gotten over the shock of being together again, our conversation, wherever it started, eventually drifted toward Mom.

You could count on it. Although they had been apart for nearly three years now, they had carried on an intermittent affair, meeting from time to time at a nice location on the coast or at a resort, something Mom always told Adele about, and she told me. There was a sort of magnetism between the two of them and, by extension, the four of us when things were going well. I see them as a pair of those little magnetic black and white Scotty dogs that were popular when I was a kid. You set them facing one another and they scoot together and lock up. Move them around and they head out in unpredictable directions, fleeing each other.

Before supper, Dad and I walked out into the thicket so he could show me Belle's gravesite. A pile of whitewashed stones stacked up waist high, like a well-constructed cairn, something you'd expect to see at a historical site. As we stood over the stones, there were the evening bird calls. The sky was red though the treetops.

Back in the kitchen, I started washing the rice for dinner. Dad sat hunched over the table with a bottle of Miller High Life. He had put on some weight, his khaki shirt stretched tight through the shoulders, his hair skimpy and losing its reddish color. I chose some words, considered them, and then without warning, asked him why he wanted me down here.

He took a moment. "It's something we'll talk about," he said. "Right now, I want a peaceful meal together. I've been cooking all afternoon."

"I bet you're seeing a woman," I said. "Right?"

He picked up the bottle and smiled. Opened his mouth and closed it and I waited for a comeback which didn't materialize. Instead, he got up and took down plates and bowls. He set a glass jar full of silverware on the table. A box of salt crackers, pickled okra, peppers, Tabasco. From the top shelf of the cabinet, he retrieved a small wooden box, egrets carved on the lid, opened it, took out paper and a cloth sack, and then started rolling a joint meticulously. I watched his artistry. He said he was tending a patch of the stuff in an old shed back behind the house. Mom was the one who planted it. We passed the joint and drank ice cold beer and, in a little while, ate a fine, spicy meal.

There was a basketball game on TV and after clearing the table, we went into the living room and sat in front of the screen with fresh beers and fuzzy minds. In time, Dad reached for the remote and killed the sound, so the players were suddenly moving up and down the court in pantomime, a silent flow of grace.

"It's like this," Dad said. "Six months ago, less, I met a man in a bar in Lafayette, downtown. A place you wouldn't know of, patronized by an older crowd. I like to go on Friday nights. They have bingo in one room and backgammon and if you can get invited, poker upstairs. We were sitting side by side at the bar. A big man, he'd make two of you or me, with a nearly bald head and a thin mustache, the kind you don't see anymore. Naturally, we started talking. That's why people go there. Before long, we were talking about religion. He's a religious man, though not one to wear it on his sleeve.

"His name's Otto Wilks and we got into this conversation. His old man had been a preacher like mine, but in Kentucky. Otto himself preached sometimes and he had the voice for it, deep and clear, a Bible voice we used to call it. Naturally, I asked him what a preacher was doing in a bar. 'Who was it turned water to wine,' he said to me, which is what you could expect him to say. He quoted the scriptures, the book of John, about the miracle at the wedding party and I added, 'But thou hast kept the good wine until now.' Seeing I wasn't ignorant of the Bible, we kept on in that vein, drinking and talking about scripture, memories coming into my head, which was like uncovering a bunch of old bones."

"A resurrection," I said with a trace of jest in my voice, which Dad didn't acknowledge.

"To make it short, Otto asked me to his church they call The Full Gospel Evangelical Tabernacle Church. Then, what he said might have seemed farfetched, except he had steady eyes and an assuring voice." Dad rubbed his jaw as if expecting to find his beard there. He breathed out. "The church is Pentecostal, charismatic, old-time believers. They practice what Jesus Christ said in the book of Mark. In Mark, he said that a true believer could take up serpents and drink any kind of poison and it won't harm them."

"He believed that?"

"He believes it, all right, and people in his church live by it."

A question I didn't expect fell on my tongue. I asked if it was something his dad had believed.

"God no. He would hate it, damn it."

"No wonder, worshiping snakes doesn't sound Christian," is what I said then.

"They don't worship snakes. Nobody worships snakes. But they take the Bible by its word. There are snakes all through the Bible. Moses in the wilderness made a bronze snake that people could look on to cure a bite. Paul shook a viper off his hand into a fire with no harm coming to him. We discussed these things, Otto and me. In any case, I went to one of the meetings out of curiosity or maybe thinking I was going to a circus. But it's nothing like you would imagine or people think they know. There's more to it," he said and paused a minute. "Look," he said, "I started this with you before I meant to. I want a little time together before we get into it."

I sat back. He closed his mouth. A silence. And then we turned our attention to the basketball game.

The Full Gospel Evangelical Tabernacle Church wasn't like anybody's idea of a tabernacle or a church. It was an old, sheet metal building, once a warehouse I would guess, set among a few silos and smaller structures alongside abandoned railroad tracks several miles north of Lafayette. When we drove up, there were a dozen cars and pickup trucks parked to one side. It was late evening, nearly dark, and a pale moon and wispy clouds floated over the tree line. The night was chilly, but Dad cracked the window a few inches anyway. He took a joint from his breast pocket. "Preparation," he said, lighting up. We sat in my car passing the joint back and forth while he told me he always had a smoke before going into the service—to lighten his spirits and level out the rest of him, he said.

We had been together two full days by this time. We had eaten well, drunk well. Dad had kept up his usual chatter, emptying his mind and digging around in mine—my love life and musical career, places I play and my finances, and what I knew about Mom and the kind of company she was keeping. I didn't tell him that she had recently visited Adele in El Paso, that she was planning to come to Vegas in the spring, how good she was looking, or the pictures and letters we were all sending back and forth.

That morning, we had taken the little skiff he had owned for years and paddled through Winslow Bayou in the wilds and swampland a short drive from the house. It was a bright, breezy day and the

water was black in the shadows of the tupelo and cypress trees that
rose into the sky like columns in a cathedral, the Spanish moss
lifting and swaying when the wind gusted. The swamp in winter is a
kinder, gentler, and far less imposing place than in the dead heat of
a Louisiana summer. You're stunned by unusual scents and shades of
green and yellow and splashes of red and the abundance of big water
birds that come down to winter. The muddy banks are dried up. The
earth is covered with pale leaves and the understory thinned out some
so in places there are distances. A lot of the snakes and other creatures
are curled in their mud holes. Wading water, we dragged the skiff up
onto dry ground under a grove of trees covered in vines.

We gathered wood and built a fire to dry our shoes and socks.
Made coffee in the old pot Dad used to carry on surveying trips.
Then, dwelled in the lull and humming silence until Dad couldn't
stand it any longer. He gripped my knee with his strong hand and
told me in all seriousness why he had to have me down here. It's not
going to happen, he told me, but in the unlikely case he got bit and
it was serious, he expected me to take care of things, whether it's the
hospital or something else. Otto's got your number, he said. You come
down quick, on an airplane this time. "Your mother and sister have
no business knowing about the church. I want you to tell them that I
got bit out here in this patch of swamp. That's what I'm asking. I don't
want them whining and complaining and damning my soul."

I bit my tongue to silence the noise in my brain. *Did he really
expect me to pull that off?* Before I opened my mouth, he stood up and
headed out into the bush, picking his way over the roots and leaves,
barefoot, so he wouldn't have to entertain my response or look into
my face for a while. I built up the fire. Half rotted wood burns fast.
Before long, he came back and I refilled his cup and mine. I wanted
to understand and sympathize, a sentiment that used to well up in me
even as a child sometimes. When he and Mom fought, which wasn't
that often, I would feel an obligation to take his side because, in the
end, he was sure to get the worst of it. Mom had a quicker mind and
wore a kind of armor that Dad had no hope of penetrating.

"On rare occasions, people get bit," he said, standing over me.
"Very rare, but I'll grant you that. A copperhead's not going to do
permanent harm and not often a rattlesnake."

"Don't be a freak, Dad. What is it? It's not what anybody would call religion, you know."

"Listen, a person can analyze this and that to a substantial death if he wants to. But I'll be damned. I'm nearly an old man and have come around to dealing with the same kind of stuff I was dealing with at twelve or thirteen. I don't know why all that's cropped back up, questioning what I should believe in is what I mean. It's the consequence of guilt from being raised in a serious church by that old man, I guess. But look, if I ever said out loud that I don't believe, I'm afraid I'd be forced to chew my tongue off."

"Seriously?"

"Seriously. I was raised with a holy fear of every word in the Bible. The fear still creeps into my head."

"What fear?"

"What do you think? Eternity."

He eased down on his butt. A grunt. A kneecap popping.

"Listen, Dad, use some common sense before you get hurt."

"You won't believe this, but in the scheme of things, I'm not all that afraid of it," he went on. "Look, I've spent my life wading swamps and thickets, fresh water, salt water. Snakes in every tree and mud hole. But, you know, after the first service I went to, I was surprised at the time I had—the music and singing and speaking in tongues that I'd never heard first hand. There was a woman, eighty-two I found out later on, and a man, her son-in-law, handling serpents while everybody was singing and praying. I got home that night, most of the night gone, exhausted, and slept a black sleep straight through, which was unusual for me then. I began considering the risk that woman, Sister Vinetta's her name, was willing to take in her worship. It started to humble me."

So after that first service, Dad kept going back. He made friends with Otto and his wife and others in the church and began to regret it when the snakes weren't brought out. The first time for him was a copperhead, he said, that belonged to the Preacher. The Preacher prayed over it, lifted it out of a cage, and laid it in his hands out in front of the pulpit.

"The major revelation was I could do it," he said. "The truth is, it was an old worn-out snake used to being handled, but there it was in my two hands accepting me. By then, I'd witnessed men and women handling two or three at a time or draped over a shoulder. That's not me. I'm not in it for show or to tempt God.

"What I do, and you'll appreciate this, is dwell on the music. Usually, there is at least a guitar and bass guitar and tambourines, often a drum set. People sing old songs, some that I recall," he smiled. "*Like a Tree Planted in Deep Water*. I bet that's one you never heard of. People start dancing, stomping the floorboards. Ribbons in the women's hair. It's a matter of giving up your will and it's a sort of wonder because you're doing something a human being's not supposed to be able to do."

"So, what makes it spiritual?"

"Well, at least it's a holy mystery," he said. "They say that the serpent is an instrument, a God made instrument…like a cypress tree. Cypress trees make their own music when a wind blows through them."

The coffee was gone. I tossed the dregs out of my cup. Dad went silent, our campfire smoke drifting toward him. He shifted around and placed the bottoms of his flat, leathery feet to the coals and smoky ash.

"But you've got to admit there's a dark side to this," I said.

"Like I told you, the permission to do it is written in red letters. People in the church believe they're fulfilling those words. Otherwise, in these times, no one will. It's that simple; they're taking on a responsibility nobody else is willing to take on. They wash one another's feet, they sing and pray half the night sometimes."

By this time, out there in the swamp, Dad had my head barely functioning and I'm not sure how well it was functioning later as we sat in my car getting a little high out in front of the tin church. Other vehicles had been arriving, their lights swinging past us. Then inside the building, the music started. At first, I could make out an acoustic guitar and a woman singing a sort of low tenor, and then, in a while, other instruments joined in like in a jam session and the sound climbed. A couple with kids and then an old man being helped along on a walker were dim figures approaching the open doorway at the side of the building. I got out of the car. I saw the red ash as Dad took a final toke and then came around to join me.

The moon was pale orange now and there was a yellow glow from windows in the building, all glorified, no doubt, by the stuff we had been consuming from Dad's secret garden.

Soon the music coming out of the metal shell was full on, something like bluegrass, a fast tempo. It was not what I would call spiritual music so much as old roadhouse music that got your spirits up. And then they started a song I was familiar with, *Take Me to the River* by Al Green, who became a preacher himself at a church in Arkansas, a song covered by a lot of respected groups and one that, in my mind, conflates baptism in a river with young sex, though I guess it depends on who's listening to it: *Take me to the river...wash me down with water, wash me in the water...cleanse my soul....* And a story unfolds which involves love, rejection, spiritual permission... lyrics that, at that moment, I was able to relate to, at least that's what my mind allowed me to think.

Dad reached out and gripped my shoulder.

I said, "I think I'll go in there with you."

"Not going to happen," he said.

I don't know what came over me. I turned and took his face in my hands just long enough to feel the weathered indentions and bristles where there used to be a beard. There's a photo of him chest high in the muck of Okefenokee Swamp holding a red and white ranging pole, for me that beard a big part of it. "I never thought you'd shave your beard," I said.

"That's another story." He smiled. "I'll tell you someday."

Then, he turned away and waved back at me to go on. As he approached the doorway, a man emerged into the rectangle of light and shook his hand. They embraced and the next thing I knew, he was part of the music.

Danny's Pool

Far off in the kitchen, the phone rang. When no one answered it, that is, when his mother didn't answer it, Randall flipped over and buried his face deep into the pillow. Breathing, then not breathing, smothering in his own stale breath and the disgusting sound of the phone while knowing for sure what was going on—his mother still upstairs in her bedroom zonked out and curled into a knot alongside Greg, Greg-what's-his-name, who had taken up residence, temporarily, two months ago.

A moment of quiet and Randall shoved the blanket back and slowly climbed out of bed, stripped off his pajama bottoms, and kicked them into a corner across the room. While scrubbing his scalp to get his mind functioning, he tried to shake off a new picture of his mother, her sometimes pretty face hidden under a bundle of scorched blond hair, as the freak sprawled beside her.

In the bathroom, Randall peed and then stood over the toilet for a while longer than necessary. He cupped his hands under the faucet, gulped water, and washed his face with a thin sliver of soap. He paused at the mirror, examining a tiny starburst of a zit that had recently appeared along one jaw. He ran a towel over his face and then a wet comb through his hair, crossed to his room, and dressed. Randall Truitt. He was fourteen.

His mother was Brenda Bissell because she had taken back her old name after his father left, though Randall sometimes called her Babs because she liked that. There was nothing to do but let her sleep it off, the alcohol or dope or whatever it was she and ol' Greg, a long, skinny guy with a buzz cut and sharp chin, had gotten into last night.

In the kitchen, Randall filled two bowls and then a plastic mixing bowl with sugar-coated cereal, poured in milk, and carried them into the living room where Justin and Ivy were sitting on the floor wedged into a little burrow between the coffee table and sofa watching cartoons. Ivy, who had a red nose and tangled yellow hair, was three and a half, Justin five. Still half asleep, they took their bowls while focused on Dora the Explorer and her pink monkey, who were on a log trying to cross a wild river. Randall sat down on the sofa among them and, grabbing the controls, flipped channels to MTV, where Shakira, singing *Loca*, suddenly lit up the screen. Justin squealed but soon got caught up in the music, the Latin rhythm, Shakira's silvery figure, her long mermaid hair. Ivy, smelling musty like the bed she slept in, rocked her head back and forth. She glanced up at Randall and then scooted over to lean back against his leg.

Halfway through his cereal, Randall heard them rumbling around upstairs, a toilet being flushed, a door closing. In a minute, Greg was standing at the top of the stairs and then slowly coming down them. He was wearing a robe closed at the neck with a fist, half smiling, and Randall could feel him about to say something or yell something, you could never tell, especially first thing in the morning. Especially when their mother was out of sight.

Randall turned the sound down. "Where's Mom?" he said to Greg. "Is she coming down?"

"Headache," Greg said, pausing near the bottom of the stairs. "She took a fall last night. Cracked it back here." He touched the back of his head.

"Justin's supposed to go to kindergarten," Randall announced like it was a challenge.

But instead of waiting for an answer, he turned up the volume, flipped to the cartoons his brother and sister were watching, and headed back into the kitchen, then on out the screen door to the small back porch. The cat scurried away, the dog came up to him, panting.

She was a white, bristle-haired mongrel with a few mud-gray spots and short, fat legs. You couldn't have invented an uglier dog, his mother's dog, found at a rescue shelter a year ago. She had named her Blondie and bought her a rhinestone collar; nobody else, not even Justin anymore, paid any attention to her. Randall let Blondie lap the last of the milk and cereal from his big plastic bowl and then replenished her food bowl and the cat's bowl from bags in the kitchen. At the outside faucet, he filled the water trough that the two animals shared.

It was a warm spring day, the sun shining over the roofline of the houses on the far side of the alley.

The phone in the kitchen rang again and the sound of the TV died; any moment now, ol' Greg would be picking up the receiver. Randall stood outside on the porch listening through the screen door, though he knew who it would be, Greg's boss or somebody else from work. He was a gluer or something like that at the plywood mill on the outskirts of their small town where there were warehouses and train tracks. One minute late and somebody would start calling.

Randall thought of going back inside to see about Justin and Ivy, to check her diaper—she was still wearing diapers part of the time. He calculated his chances of getting past Greg without interference and on down the hall to his bedroom without encountering his mother so he could retrieve his books, homework, shoes. Greg was laughing into the phone now, working on the person at the other end of the line.

It wasn't worth it. Confronting Greg right then seemed worse than anything that might happen later on, though there was nothing he'd like better than to smash the guy's face in. In jeans and a short-sleeved shirt, barefoot and empty handed, Randall crossed the backyard and climbed the chain link fence by wedging his toes between the sharp metal links, lifting himself over the spikes on top and dropping into the alley. He had long legs and strong, loopy arms, a stout chest that caused the maroon shirt to tighten in front when he stood up straight.

On tender feet, he made his way in thin sunlight down the alley past garbage bins and trash, a barking Schnauzer, and open garages, to East Lavender Street, up Lavender to Payton, and then two more blocks where he turned toward Danny Sedgwick's house. They were friends, not great friends, but classmates since grade school. Now in their first year of high school, Randall sometimes helped him with his homework and they were partners during the biology lab. A lot of mornings he would meet Danny in front of his house and they would walk up to the corner to catch the school bus together.

The Sedgwicks had a nice, big house of red and black bricks and tall windows. There were flowers in Mexican pots on the front porch and a new pool in back that Danny had been talking about. Approaching the house, Randall often thought about what it would be like to live there, not in that particular house necessarily, but one like it, him and Babs and Justin and Ivy, and on a nice street like Danny's street. Randall had daydreams like that from time to time but, of course, didn't go so far as to fool himself about it.

The doorbell was a chime that seemed to float on air.

The door opened slightly and then wider. It was Danny's mother. "I'm afraid he's gone already," she said. "I think he tried to call you to offer a ride. His father drove him this morning."

"Oh, shit," Randall said, then glanced up into her face. "I'm sorry."

"That's okay." She opened the door wider. "Are you all right?"

Randall didn't say anything.

"Where are your shoes?"

"They're…I mean, they're at home."

"Is something wrong?"

"Yeah, a little," he said but without conviction.

"Anyway, you're here and probably missed the bus," she said, after a short silence. She looked him up and down. "No books? Come on. Come in a minute."

He followed her through the entrance hall past the dark living room and into a big kitchen where suddenly there was a lot of light. Everything smelled fresh and clean. Danny's mother leaned back against the sink and crossed her arms under her breasts. She was wearing white Bermuda shorts and a nice, pink shirt. Her legs were tan and she was barefoot with painted toenails.

"Now, what about your shoes?" she asked him.

Randall said again that they were at home and when she asked him why, he crossed his arms like she had crossed hers and told her that he shouldn't talk about it right now.

"Is there some trouble?"

"Not much," he said.

"Not much?"

"It's all right."

"So, did you come by to borrow some shoes for school?"

"Well, I thought about Danny. Maybe."

"Jesus. What size do you wear?" She was looking at his feet and he could feel his toes twitching and was ashamed of them, long and naked, of his hair uncut for a while and probably sticking out over his ears, of his whole appearance, which suddenly didn't seem to belong in this nice house. To make it worse, Mrs. Sedgwick frowned and then turned away and opened the refrigerator. She got a glass and poured grape juice into it, placed it on the bar that ran halfway across the kitchen.

"I want you to sit down and drink that," she said. "Okay?" Weakly, she smiled at him. He sat on a bar stool and drank the grape juice, which was ice cold, tingly, not quite sweet enough. She left and, in a few minutes, came back with shoes, rather worn white canvas sneakers and also bright white socks.

"See if you can wear these, but first you have to tell me what's the matter. What happened?"

Randall found that he really didn't want the sneakers or to tell her anything, but now it seemed an obligation to come up with something that would please her. Slowly, as he pulled on one sock and then the other, he began to relate, as the truth, what he imagined could have taken place last night with his mother and Greg, this "guy" is what he called Greg, and what he had learned this morning—that his mother had taken a fall. She might have broken something, he continued, embellishing the story, and then, to make it more real, he said there could be something wrong with her head. "Greg's a dope," he said. And then, sitting the glass on the counter, added—a dealer. "Maybe he deals," he said, correcting himself, because all at once he realized that Mrs. Sedgwick was giving him her full attention, her blue eyes coaxing him on, and he didn't want to lose it. He had never really talked with her, or any woman like her, and now he could see that she was interested in him. A warmth that seemed to come from her swept through him, promising a closer relationship. It was something like slipping on a warm sweater that might keep out the cold.

"I've met your mother at the school," he heard her say. "She seemed like a nice person." She paused. "She's okay, isn't she? Does she need help, do you think?"

"No. I don't know."

"Did you see her up and walking around?"

"Not exactly. Later on, she was having some trouble talking."

"Oh, god. Look, honey, you should probably call someone, 911. That's the thing to do to be sure she's okay. There's no use in taking a chance."

He glanced at the telephone sitting on a phone book at the end of the bar.

"Not here," she said, at once. "You want to keep this in your own family. You should call from home or if you don't want to go home right now, from the K.C. Quick Stop up on Hudnall. They have a pay phone. Tell them what you told me and ask them to go to your house and check on things. The police and medics too, say that. They'll want to do that anyway. It's their job."

"I don't know," Randall said, a little flabbergasted.

"Do you have any money?"

He got down from the bar stool and into his pockets, one after the other, and showed her—two dimes, some pennies.

She disappeared again and came back and led him to the front door where she gave him a dollar bill unfolded from her coin purse. Then, she thought a moment and came up with two more dollars, one for the pay phone and city bus to school and the rest for lunch, she said. "Go, go, go," she said, and then clutched his shoulders. "Hon, listen to me, don't tell anybody where you got that, okay. Or that you even talked to me. I wouldn't want them, Greg, your mother's friend, to know about that. Do you understand?" She took his face in her long fingers and, in a fragrant cloud, planted a kiss on his forehead, then wiped it off with her thumb.

It was two blocks to West Hudnall and then another up Hudnall, which was filled with morning traffic, to the K.C. Quick Stop. Inside, he asked the lady at the counter for change and then went to the back of the store and stood in front of the payphone beside cases of beer. After a moment, it occurred to him that he had no intention of calling 911 or any place else. Following Mrs. Sedgwick's instructions had been automatic, to satisfy her and string out the story he had told. He touched the spot on his forehead where she'd kissed him, sure that if he looked into a mirror, he would find lipstick from her lips there.

On the bus, Randall kept glancing down at the white shoes, frayed around the top but bright like the socks, as if they had both

been bleached. They were a size or so too large for him and flopped
a little when he walked. Not Danny's shoes, he realized. They might
have been his father's shoes, Leland. That was Danny's father's name
and her name was Camille. He knew quite a lot about Danny's
family. His sister, Natalie, a fifth grader, had recently won a photo
contest; her picture of three rotting peaches was being displayed in
the town library, Danny said. He said that rotting was what makes
them creative, bragging about it. Their new pool was eight feet in
the deep end and could be heated in winter, but there was no diving
board. Leland wore a tie to work in an office in a building on the
town square. He was slightly plump and exactly the same height as
his wife, which Danny thought was neat. Some Sundays, they rode
bicycles together, the whole family, around the lake at Sherman Park.
Without trying, Randall's mind imagined how appealing Danny's
mother would be pumping a bicycle in her white Bermuda shorts.

The bus dropped him at the corner of the athletic field, where a
large number of girls in gym shorts were playing kickball, two games
going on. He waited behind a row of bleachers for the class to end and
the coach to leave so he could walk on up to the school building and get
inside without being harassed. He had never asked himself until now, this
moment, why he was going to school today in the first place, except he
hardly ever missed class or failed to do his homework, though now his
homework was on the floor beside his bed. He had learned, long ago, it
was easier to go ahead and do it on time than put up with the hassles.
Besides, homework took his mind off other things and, for some reason,
he liked pleasing his teachers and being called on in class.

His grades were good, he showed discipline—teachers often said
that. There had been a conference not long ago where Mr. Harden, the
assistant principal, and Miss Huff, the geometry teacher, had talked to
him about college. If he would buckle down and keep up the good work,
he was college material. There were scholarships for students like him,
Mr. Harden said, in fact, almost promised. He pulled out a chart that
showed what a difference college would make in his life, a million dollars
or something like that, which later had made Randall consider Ivy and
Justin and get a glimpse of the future where he would have the money
to get them into college, too. The possibility played in his head and,
though not completely believing it, he had a hopeful feeling about it.

Going up the hill toward a backdoor that opened into the cafeteria, the bell suddenly rang out, clanging like a warning, which seemed to change the chemistry in his brain. No books, no homework. His breath probably stank and he didn't want Danny to see him walking around in his father's old shoes. Then, as a group of kids were emerging from the cafeteria door, Randall stopped short, turned and took off running.

A long time later, at Long John Silver's on West Jefferson, he went inside and ordered the whitefish sandwich with cheese, $2.63, and water. With thirty-two cents left in his pocket, he sat on a curb in the parking lot under the sun and meager clouds and gazed at the wooded hills south of town and slowly ate the sandwich, barely tasting it. Without school, there was nothing whatsoever to do or think about that he wanted to think about. He started out again in the general direction of home. After a while, he passed through a small, deserted park where there was a fountain lined with crumbling concrete. The fountain was filled with black, sour water littered with rotted leaves and peelings and rusted cans. Looking closer, Randall was startled by two dead goldfish, with bloated eyes, floating on their sides. Some kid or crazy person must have dumped them in there. He stared for a moment and spit into the water.

Beyond the park, he crossed the empty field where the county fair set up when it came through town and continued along a street of one-story office buildings and warehouses—once thinking briefly of his mother, of Babs, sitting at the kitchen table in the silky housecoat she wore around the house. She would be on the telephone talking to her friend, Margery, drinking a diet Pepsi while marking job announcements in a newspaper. At supper time, Greg would pull up into the driveway—and Randall clinched his teeth, as his lungs expanded and then collapsed with the pure uncertainly of what was going to happen then, what would be said about him skipping out without a word.

Still, he kept walking toward home, the canvas shoes rubbing a hot spot on one of his heels, the sun zapping his eyes every time it slipped from behind a cloud and, after a while, he ended up in a neighborhood pointed toward Danny's house. He was drawn toward it and just kept on walking, entertaining the idea that he needed to thank Mrs. Sedgwick for the shoes, the money.

The doorbell chimed. He waited and pushed the button again. At last, as he was about to give up, Danny's mother came to the door just as before, in the white Bermuda shorts, except her short, blondish hair was combed back wet now like she had been in the shower or maybe the pool.

"I brought you your shoes." He held them up, the socks tucked inside. He felt utterly deflated but held himself together and presented the shoes to her, shoes that were soiled now from the mud beside the leaking fountain and his sweaty feet.

"What are you doing here? Didn't you go to school?" she asked, gazing at him and ignoring the shoes.

"Yeah," he said quickly and then explained that Mr. Harden had given him a ride over here.

"He did?"

"Yeah, he said it's okay if I really needed to go home to check on Mom."

Chewing her bottom lip, Mrs. Sedgwick opened the door on out.

"What did they say when you called?"

Randall tried to get that question into his clogged head.

"911, the police?"

"Oh, yeah. They said they're going to go over there to check," he said. "And then my mother, she's okay." He almost mentioned Ivy, Justin, but probably she didn't know they existed.

"Well, you did the right thing. Look, take those with you," she said, "the shoes and socks, too, and then sometime when you're by here, you can leave them on the porch."

Randall felt better now, relieved. He'd done the right thing and she looked satisfied and he recalled how she had smelled when she pressed her lips to his forehead that morning, the scent of something in her hair.

Randall touched his throat and swallowed. "Can I have a drink of water?" he asked.

"Water, okay." She stepped back to let him in.

In the kitchen, it was as if time had hardly passed at all since he had been here this morning, the room shiny and filled with light. The same clean fragrance, everything fixed in its place. Without being invited, he sat down at the bar on the same high stool as before. His stool.

"Can I have grape juice instead?" He asked her.

"Grape juice?"

"Instead of water, I mean. It was really good."

She hesitated and then opened the refrigerator door, which was littered with photos and notes and colorful gadgets holding them in place. One of the photos was of Danny in swimming goggles, bent forward laughing. She found a glass and poured it half full from the same bottle as this morning.

"Mrs. Sedgwick, can I ask you something?"

As she handed him the glass, a nice feeling went through him, as if some part of him was becoming accustomed to this place, which wasn't so scary anymore.

"Is your husband's name Leland?"

"Leland, yes. That's his name, but Mr. Sedgwick is better."

"I was wondering where he works, what profession." It seemed an adult thing to ask.

"Well, he works in sales. He markets things, medical supplies and equipment." She stepped back against the sink and crossed her arms and legs, too, this time. She peered at him.

"Do you mean like medicine and x-ray machines?"

"Well, not those things exactly."

"He must be successful."

"He works hard."

"Because he wants to buy you all nice things." He wanted her to continue talking, to think he was worth talking with here in her house. But she tilted her head, her voice changed. "That's not something that we need to talk about."

"Why?"

"Why? We just don't," she said, spacing the words out. "Besides, I'm busy. I want you to finish the juice and take the shoes and go outside and put them on."

"Well, I was wondering if you've been in the pool." Randall was looking across at her hair.

"That's right."

"Can I go swim first, just till Danny gets home?"

"Right now, you need to go to your own home, hear? The pool is for the family. Now it's time to go, to see about your mother."

"I've been walking a long way." He set the glass down, a thud on the bar.

"I thought Mr. Harden brought you."

Randall weighed her words but didn't say anything.

"Did you tell the truth about that?"

"Am I too sweaty for the pool?" He blurted to avoid the question.

"Oh, my god. Come on. I've been nice. You lied to me and now I don't know what to believe and this is a little strange. Drink up and leave. Do you understand?"

Randall didn't move. His confusion wouldn't let him move. She started toward him and then, as if changing her mind, left the kitchen. He heard the front door open and she called his name, two, three times. He touched his face, the tiny bump along his jaw, and felt that it must be larger and redder now because his skin was heating up. Then leaving the stool, he wiped his nose with the back of his hand. He went down the hall and, as he slipped past her through the half-opened doorway, she looked away.

Outside in the yellow sunlight, slightly dazed, he gathered himself, and finally, with his knees feeling weak and short of breath, started at an angle across the front lawn. All at once, she called out from the porch. As he turned back, the shoes came flying at him, first one, then the other, and the socks sailing free like startled birds darting into the air. The shoes landed a few feet apart, the socks further away, and for some reason, some dumb, automatic reason, Randall dropped to his knees and crawled around over the thick, spongy grass, gathering them up. Then, he held them protected against his chest, while up on the porch, she disappeared back into the house.

But it wasn't over, he couldn't leave it there, kneeling like a creep in her grass. Slowly, he stuffed the socks into the shoes. He stood and carried them around to the back of house and dumped them in the driveway. In front of him was a high wooden fence, the gate pulled shut. It was locked. He breathed in, exhaled. The fence reached well above his head, but for him, pulling himself over it was no trouble. He landed with his bare feet in a bed of pansies and stepped over onto warm concrete, an apron around the pool. The pool was smaller than he had imagined it might be; the water, however, gleamed like a polished lens, magnifying the bottom, which seemed so close you could reach down and touch it. At one end, a waterfall poured out from a separate little pool into the big one.

With little hesitation, Randall removed his shirt and stripped to his boxer shorts, so intense now it didn't matter that they were gray, shapeless. He kneeled at the edge of the pool and slipped like a lizard into the chilly, pale green water. Immediately, it was over his head, and he came up gasping, spitting, and then treading. He pushed his wet hair back out of his eyes. A few strokes toward one end and he found the bottom and almost instantly heard the patio door slide open. At first, she didn't say a word. She came slowly out from under a porch roof into the sunlight and crossed her arms and raised her chin slightly, as if to make herself appear taller.

Randall looked up, waiting.

"You little shit," she blurted out, her face tightening and suddenly growing quite ugly. But she didn't cuss again or demand that he get out of the pool or say anything else. Instead, she took up a long, plastic pole with a dipper on one end and came across the concrete toward him. "Out, out, out," she blurted and then screamed and began jabbing at him as if wielding a spear.

*Jab...jab...jab...*the end of the pole flashed in his face, struck the side of his head, and he latched onto it. They wrestled like that for a moment and he gathered his strength and suddenly jerked with all his fury and she came tumbling into the pool, head first. She rose up flailing, choking, trying to catch her breath but having trouble like her throat was clogged. He got to her and from there it was easy, hardly anything to it...pounding her head, her ears, her distorted face when it appeared, beating the knuckles of his fists against bone and flesh, half-blinded by water splashing into his eyes. He tangled his fingers into her hair and leaned back, dragging her down, and on down. She continued kicking, but the rest of her body seemed to be paralyzed, helpless. The thrashing ceased and before long, her bare, still feet drifted up near the surface of the water. Still, he held her. And a sense of astonishment overtook him, a disbelief, a wonder at how easily she had succumbed to him.

Turkeys

Early that morning, a whistling norther had attacked the woods and thickets, the wind tearing at the treetops, ice crystals collecting in the clumps of pine needles and gullies and along the muddy banks of bogs and cypress sloughs. In the late afternoon, two men stumbled up out of the bush and dark trees onto an old wagon road. They wore canvas hunting jackets and thick neck scarfs and billed caps with ear flaps, shotguns broken down and game bags hanging loose and empty from their shoulders. They were a retired building contractor and local politician named Withers and his neighbor, Fred Connor, whose investment firm handled a healthy portion of Withers' insurance and retirement accounts.

The two men were bottom weary and freezing, soaked wet up to their knees. At dawn, they had left Connor's car, a pale blue Buick, out in front of a little tin-roofed country church, which was somewhere up this road, or so Connor said, kept saying, as they trudged on around one wooded bend to the next as the old road deteriorated to a trail and then not much more than a footpath.

There was a turkey to blame for this. A few hours ago, they had gotten turned around chasing it up out of a creek bed. "A tom," Connor had hollered when the bird burst from the undergrowth like angry thunder. As soon as Withers had let loose his first shot, Connor called out, "I believe you hit him, he's got a gimp wing."

The bird, in fact, flew a crazed pattern under the canopy, landed on a high branch, and proceeded from one tree to another, squawking and croaking, *tut, tut, tutting*...leading them on. Then it would settle, displaying that one droopy wing just long enough for Withers to raise the barrel of his shotgun, which seemed to be a signal to the turkey to take off again.

Soon enough, the surly creature had them scrambling through vines and bush and before long, the hunters were slogging through a bog overrun with gallberry and water tupelo and some sort of thorny shrub that tore at their jackets and freezing fists. Connor, who had hunted these thickets before and had brought his prized client here with the promise of a Christmas turkey, led the way, pausing each time the bird lit. "Take a shot," he'd whisper, "he's yours now." And Withers would let go a barrel or two only to see the bird tumble into the void, spread the one good wing and hobbled one, and sail away with the jerky grace of a freed-up kite.

"I want that bastard," Withers muttered after the fourth or fifth attempt, expending nearly a dozen magnum tungsten shells. In his anxious mind, he could see the wild bird stuffed with his wife's cornbread-walnut dressing, resting on her bone china platter in the middle of their Christmas table, surrounded by admiring friends and family. "He's yours," Connor kept saying in his annoying voice until, at last, they found themselves in a field of chest high grass and discovered there wasn't one, but now two gray-speckled birds sitting at a distance side-by-side on the branch of a lone bare tree, the plump creatures gobbling and grousing with one another.

To get a sure shot, the men crouched down and slowly crawled on hands and knees through the deep weeds. Withers took a bandana and wiped his spectacles and then spots of blood where the marsh thorns had chewed on his face. Whispering a solemn oath, he suddenly popped up shooting, but not before the two birds had dropped away, and then, circling once, headed toward a distant tree line. Withers ran stumbling and reloading while Connor huffed close behind. They crossed a once plowed field, passed through a stand of hardwoods trailing Spanish moss, and then, at last, a prickly hedgerow that dumped them out onto the old, pitted wagon road.

∾

As the road petered out to a footpath, the woods thinned and opened up. The broad sky, visible now for the first time in a while, was a pale, sullen blue-gray with clouds spread east to west. Flakes of snow were drifting in the frigid air. As they crossed a footbridge over a narrow creek, the silence of the woods was suddenly broken.

"I been waitin' on y'all." An old man stood just ahead beside the trail. He was short, hardly taller than a fencepost, wore bib overalls over a flannel shirt, and under a crushed felt hat was a small, round, red face set flat on what seemed the broadest shoulders either man had ever seen. In other words, a box of a man on two stout trunks.

"What's that?" Connor asked the old man.

"He said he was waiting for us," Withers said. "You sure you mean us?"

"For a good while now," the old man answered, eying their game bags. "You fellers do a lot of shootin'."

Withers produced a smile, suddenly realizing they had found someone who surely knew the way out of there. "Not much luck today," he said, trying to make light of it. "It's hard as hell to get a decent shot in all that undergrowth and the cold don't help either."

Withers lifted the shotgun off of his shoulder just to emphasize that he had it, an expensive one, too, though there wasn't, in his mind, anything menacing going on here. He told the old man they were on the way out of the woods. "There's a little church somewhere near here," he went on. "Maybe you could point out the way to get there."

"New Jerusalem. Hardly any preaching goes on there now. On occasion meetings and funerals, though."

Withers stepped up to introduce himself. He extended his hand.

The old man didn't move a muscle.

Which struck Connor as rude or maybe arrogant. "Like he said," Connor announced, trying to mix some authority into his voice, "we were just leaving to go back home and would appreciate it if you'd give us some directions to that church."

"Nope."

There was a moment of shocked silence. The flakes had turned crystalline, more sleet than snow now.

"Look here—," Connor raised his voice, causing Withers to step forward and shut him up.

"I'm sure you can understand," Withers offered politely, "that we've got a long drive ahead of us and it's getting late."

"Back to Houston," Connor said.

The old man put his large hands into his pockets. "You all come on to the house. Oma is boiling a pot a coffee for you."

"Coffee. Now, that's a kind offer. Very kind, Mr...?"

"It'll be Cotswold."

"Mr. Cotswold. But you know there's a good chance the roads will be icing up this evening. We ought to be going on our way before it gets bad."

But the old man had already retreated and was making his way up a slope through a growth of beech trees, their copper-brown leaves clicking in the breeze.

"Stubborn old fart," Connor uttered under his breath.

"Probably he just wants company," Withers said, "or maybe a few dollars. Humor him so we can get the hell out of here."

A woman in a long, faded dress was waiting on the deep front porch of an old board house, not much more than a cabin really. As they came up, she was smiling and pleasant looking, with a moon face, bright little eyes, and fine, well-placed wrinkles as some artist might depict them in a cheerful painting.

"You two've been shooting up a racket," she said, looking down on them. Lifting a big black coffee pot, she poured steaming coffee into tin cups which sat on the porch rail. She handed the cups down to her husband who passed them on to Connor and then Withers, finally taking one for himself.

"Albert's here in the barn and about give out," the woman said to her husband.

"Well, we'll go around back," the old man announced to his visitors. He turned and, with no explanation offered, led the two reluctant, impatient men around to the back of the house.

There were outbuildings—a chicken coop, an empty animal pen. Beyond the pen, two black cows with white faces and sharp horns came out of a copse of trees, as if to see who had come to visit. Beyond the yard was a barn, which was quite tall, sturdy, though patched here and there with squares and rectangles of rusted tin.

Withers asked about the cows.

"Around here, we let'em range wild," the old man said. "They come back in when it's time to eat or one needs milking."

Already the rich coffee, floating tiny grounds that wanted to get between their teeth, was announcing itself to Withers and Connor.

"Some coffee," Withers said to the old man Cotswold, aiming to make it a compliment, the way a practiced politician can without any sign of compromising himself.

"It's her wild chicory and mash," Cotswold said. "Once down your throat, it warms but won't rue back on you." He cupped his free hand around his mouth and called out to his wife. The falling snow was sparse now and gentle like down feathers.

The old woman emerged from the back door of the house with a tow sack and the big coffee pot to replenish their cups, each of the men pausing to take what she offered. A minute later, they were standing inside a wire pen behind the barn, surrounded by turkeys, six or seven of them. Some were peering out from nests built in shelves against the barn, the others gobbling and pecking at the earth or pausing to indulge their curiosity concerning the strangers. The old woman, bundled in a thick cloth coat and knit hat, began gobbling and cooing, slinging kernels of corn and seed from the burlap bag.

"Their ancestors were all wild at one time or the other," the old man said, tossing the dregs of his coffee. "They're fattened up on corn and good kitchen feed now. Ya'll go ahead, look around and take your pick."

Withers straightened his back. "Our pick?" he repeated, amused. "Mr. Cotswold, I take it you're in business, then. The turkey business."

"In a manner of speaking."

"And I guess you have in mind selling each of us one of these turkeys."

The old man lifted the coffee pot that sat handy on top of a fence post, offered it up, and then filled his cup.

"Look here," Connor said sharply. "You ought to know that we didn't come here all this way to *buy* a turkey."

"I imagine."

"But then, there you were waiting for us to come up the trail like you were expecting us," Withers said, good-naturedly now.

"It's the natural way out of the bottom once you started up the road," Cotswold said, after a sip of coffee.

"And you figured we'd be empty handed. What made you think that?" Connor asked, straining to keep it friendly.

"Albert," the old woman answered. She flung a fist of grain in a wide arc and gestured up toward the roof of the barn. Stepping back, the two men shaded their eyes against the snow and looked up. There was a bird perched there on the ridgeline of the roof, a turkey. Its long neck was erect, tail feathers fanned out and one wing lifted, as if to catch the falling snow. The other wing was extended at a raked angle.

"By god," Connor burst out. "I believe that's the one in the woods."

"Yep. Once Albert's back home, you can figure that directly some hunter's going to come along," the old woman explained.

"Chasing after him," the old man added.

"Chasing?" Withers was trying to get this straight in his head. He paused to sip coffee, calculating how to deal with this foolishness without provoking either of them.

"We saw that bird, all right," Connor said, provoked. "It's crippled."

The old man shook his head, a solemn gesture. "He caught some birdshot once when hardly more than a pup. Oma took him in and nursed him and she trained him up after that."

"Trained him?"

"To watch out for shotguns mostly and loonies stomping through the thickets. And to light high up in a tree where he can see to duck and run, run and duck, turn on a nickel when he needed to. That's some of what she taught him," the old man said.

"You expect us to believe that," Connor let out. "Everybody knows turkeys are dumb as sin."

"No sir," the old woman said firmly. "They're like a human or a dog or anything else. You find a smart one and treat'em like their smart, they're smart."

Cotswold grinned. "It don't matter. She can teach anything on two legs, four either."

"I don't know why, but that's the way it is with my sister, too. Communicating with animals is particular to us," the woman said with a lilt in her voice that made it sound logical.

Connor was beginning to fluster, exacerbated by the fix he had led his client into, but maybe more so by the home brew in the old woman's coffee, which was going straight to his head.

"Do you expect us to believe that turkey led us here?" he got out, trying to gaze into the woman's stubborn eyes.

Withers grabbed Connor's shoulder. "You've said enough," his voice rose. Then he laughed, shaking his head. "Look, all they're after is to sell us dumb city hunters a turkey. Correct?" he said, turning his gaze from Connor to the old man.

"Less you want a go back home just the way you left it," the old man said and then added, "That'll be all right, too."

"They're trying to trick us," Connor said into Withers' face.

Withers snorted. "Close your damn mouth for a while," he said, then turned to Cotswold. "Mr. Cotswold I'd like to hear what you have to offer. It's business. So how much is it for one of those turkeys?"

"I say let's go."

"Shut up," Withers snapped. "You wouldn't know where to go or have the sense to get there if you did know." Then, back to the old man, "Well, sir."

"The littler ones, they're about fifty."

Withers's head jerked back.

Connor bellowed.

Withers threw a hand up to quiet him. "Mr. Cotswold," he said, "are you aware that a person can purchase a turkey plucked and cleaned in any supermarket in Houston or anywhere else for fifteen or sixteen dollars?"

"Well, sir. I don't aspect you'd want a go home with a plucked turkey in your game pouch."

"We're not fool enough to pay fifty," Connor muttered.

"Well, these are God-raised turkeys, not grocery store turkeys, and they've been fed the way a Christmas turkey ought to be."

What the hell is God-raised, Withers started ask but didn't, as a flock of half-formed thoughts raced through his head.

"That's for the little ones," the old man went on. "The big ones, they're forty."

"Just a minute." Withers felt a jolt. "You are telling me the small ones are fifty dollars. The big ones like that one over there in the corner are forty U.S. dollars."

"That doesn't make sense." Connor's face was blooming.

"Unless you think on it a minute," the old man said.

Almost immediately, Withers's brain lit up. He shook his head slowly. "So, comparing one thing to another, you're saying the big ones are a bargain."

"And you can get two for eighty-five," the old man said.

Withers paused to calculate. "Five dollars more," he said slowly. "You have a funny kind of arithmetic, Mr. Cotswold."

"Not me," the old man said. "Oma prices'em."

Withers shook his head, half smiling in appreciation of this old couple's gall, as only an affluent businessman who had turned many a half-crooked deal in his favor could. And in that moment, he thought of the long, cold, wet, muddy, bruising chase through the tickets, the turkey magically taking wing at calculated moments. He held his cup out, asking Mrs. Cotswold for another spot of her coffee and then ordered Connor to take some more, too. At once, a light-headed warmth spread through Withers; a renewed vision of his Christmas table appeared, his wife's smile, candlelight, the holly wreath their grandkids made every year. As he wandered out of the hog wire pen into the farmyard, he sighed, reveling in a moment of self-satisfaction and rare spiritual delight.

It was half an hour through deepening shadows and thickly falling snow to the little country church. Withers's shotgun shouldered and his game bag hung warm and heavy across his ample belly. Connor's bag was full, too, though rather than walking, he seemed to float some inches off the ground from the third cup of the sweet woman's coffee. It was, overall, an easy and festive trek, Albert having been dispatched to lead the way.

We Recruits in Granny Pearl's Army

"Once a person's dead, they're either put in the ground or else burnt to ashes, so you end up dirt or smoke, one assigned to the earth, the other rising to heaven." This is what Granny Pearl told us children while sitting in the porch swing, sipping black tea, contemplating her imminent demise on that stricken Sunday afternoon. My cousin Juliette, who was six and not yet weaned from her big mouth, had asked her the question about dying, Granny Pearl's dying, what was going to happen when she died, because of something she had overheard the grownups, still inside around the dining table, talking about. "Where are we going to put her, which plot?" Juliette said they said, scooping her yellow dress up under her bottom as she sat down on the top porch step so she could look up directly into Granny Pearl's deeply webbed, vaguely oriental eyes.

"What does that mean, plot?"

There were pale oleanders blooming in the yard, red and yellow rose buds coming to life along either side of the stone path out to the front gate.

Granny Pearl spent a long moment contemplating her teacup.

"Which plot? No plot," she proclaimed at last, ignoring the crux of Juliette's question. Then, she said that about dirt and smoke.

"Now, which one would you settle for?" She pointed a long finger at me, the second oldest. "Tied to the earth or rising to heaven?"

She'd caught me off-guard.

"Tied to the earth or rising?" she repeated impatiently as she often did when encouraging one of us to offer an opinion.

When I still didn't answer right off, she poked her narrow eyes at Lucas, eleven, the oldest and by far the biggest among us.

"Heaven, I guess." Lucas nodded his burr head and crossed his arms like he was the first to solve one of Granny Pearl's riddles.

Granny Pearl turned back on me.

"I like it right here just fine," I heard my voice say.

"Just fine? The earth? Dirt?"

"Yes, ma'am."

"What of the rest of you all, dirt or smoke?"

And one by one she had each of the others choose—Charlene, my age and with fine yellow hair parted down the middle, and then the younger ones, Lisa and Ezra and then Juliette—all standing or sitting nice and clean and hair oiled or brushed in place in their Sunday outfits.

Heaven, they each said or whispered in turn, all except Juliette, who we could see was taking this about death hard, getting upset, and twisting her slightly freckled face into a red turnip while seeming to age ten years.

"You have to choose, I'm waitin'," Granny Pearl said to her, showing no mercy. "One day, you're going to die like the rest of us. It's a law of nature. Everything living dies. Something your parents probably never taught you."

She looked around and then directly at me. "Frank, I want you to think about it till your ears ache."

Granny Pearl steadied the swing with her crooked, bare toes on the porch boards, set the teacup on a little table beside the swing, and rose. Grasping the top of Juliette's curly head to brace herself, she eased down the stone steps and made her way along the path between the parade of rosebuds out to the fence, a sturdy picket fence, though in need of whitewashing. She stood alone, a surprisingly gaunt but still upright figure in a loose, plum-dark witch's dress and sparse silver-white hair spun into a knot with a lacquered wooden pin through it, gazing across the road to the pasture, which was, as far as we could see, all nettles and choke weed and tall, brown stalks of dried sunflowers lying under a cream-blue sky.

She waited, knowing we would soon come and join her. And, of course, like always we did, one after the other until all six of us were gathered round like a brood of ducklings, straining to see what she was seeing, which was, in my mind, some sort of vision we were not yet meant to understand. You see, we were, against all conventional wisdom, drawn to Granny Pearl, our grandmother (step-grandmother, to be precise), as surely as she had enveloped us in a spell, a spell you had to be a child of her heart to fully grasp and succumb to, I suppose.

There was no coddling in her, but she spoke to us like we were significant of ourselves and listened to us with her dark, glassy eyes and her large ears pitched forward, taking in every child-word like it was something worth considering.

In other words, she was nothing like normal adults, our parents and other grandparents, aunts and uncles, and lesser relatives who would show up at the "family place" for these get-togethers from time to time. In fact, it came to me at some point in my childhood that Granny Pearl had little in common with any of them. You could see an impatience and even mild disdain propping up some of her remarks and sharp glances.

"Come on in and find your own way around and don't bother with me," was one thing I had heard her say to one or another of them after accepting a dry peck on the cheek. You'd think that a child wouldn't notice such things, but the minute we stepped into her rambling old house with its storybook smells of dead lives lived and wood smoke and dark, musky corners, I would be caught up in the mystery of it all, or at least feel it. I suspected others of us children, my cousins, did as well, even the younger ones. Juliette, for instance.

Typically, the women, my mother included, scattered through the downstairs rooms to take inventory of the brocade fabrics and rubbed furniture, heirloom rugs, a pair of brass birdcages free of birds, a menagerie of figurines and bric-a-brac—ceramic animals, storybook houses, little Dutch children gazing at you. Old studio photos in thick frames on the walls, arranged in glass-fronted hutches in the living room and hallways and back in the library, which was lit with standing lamps and lined with our deceased grandfather's leather-bound law books.

Meanwhile, after the men entered and paid their respects, they would make their way to the back porch, which Granny Pearl called the *gallery*. They gathered there under the low roof and smoked and discussed the stock market and the value of things like real estate and whatever sport was in season and snuck bourbon into their coffee cups. Snuck because Granny Pearl didn't allow hard liquor inside the house and they had just as soon she didn't know they were drinking out on the gallery either.

Generally, as soon as we got home from church, which was a tradition, we children would run out back to swing in the chinaberry and persimmon trees and when that grew tiresome or a shoving match erupted, we headed for the long dead peach orchard. It was a square acre populated by withered, diseased trees turned black and knobby but rising out of spidery patches of weeds and wildflowers in spring and autumn. And then, there were the empty pens and corrals long out of use and on the edge of the front pasture a huge, old barn to explore.

There is no telling how long it had been since it housed a farm animal, but inside, where traces of sunlight came through chinks in the plank walls, was an armory of dusty farm implements and the deep aroma of dried cow dung and burlap feed sacks and things of long-ago significance. In the loft were the remnants of hay bales and back in the corners, the remains of peanut vines and rat nests and scattered feathers. Granny Pearl told us that the best feathers came from a screech owl that had shown up for many years nearly every Monday night and might again one day because certain owls could live a very long life. We'd climb the ladder and romp around up there, disturbing ghosts until someone yelled *rat* or *snake*, sending everybody scrambling down the ladder.

The women prepared dinner amidst chatter and powerful kitchen smells and shooed us to the table about half past one. Never much later.

On this defiant and amazed Sunday afternoon, Granny Pearl ate hardly anything of the meal, which the grownups kept pushing on her in the same way they pushed greens and turnips on us children. Instead, she picked at her plate with a knife in one hand, a fork in the other, drank her black tea, had a slice of cherry cake and, about the time the rest of us were half done, rose without a word and retired to the front porch.

That day, there were seven or eight grownups at the table, including my father and mother, my cousins' parents, and Mr. Whittle, a big-headed old man with short arms and a barrel belly. He once owned the bank in town and had taken care of Granny Pearl's books and affairs ever since our grandfather, Walter Beale, died, which was, I believe, nine or ten years before. Mr. Whittle nearly always followed us home from church in an ancient black car for reasons I never understood, except he was the one called on to say the blessing.

"What did I tell you?" my Aunt Francine, Lucas and Charlene's mother, said the minute Granny Pearl was out of earshot.

"She doesn't weigh ninety pounds...." Uncle Claude, who had a patchy alcoholic face, went on.

What I knew is what my mother had told me on the long drive up here to northeast Texas—three or more hours, most of it through small towns and blue-green pastures and commercial forest land—from where we lived on the outskirts of Houston. She said that Granny Pearl had gotten a bad report. "Don't say anything about it and don't be surprised when you see her if she looks different," my mother added with a smile that crept from grave to gentle.

"Or acts crazier than ever," my father said from behind the wheel. "Not crazy, forget I said crazy, but they say her mind's failing her, along with everything else. Ninety-three. This thing the doctor found is just helping it along."

"It's something they found in her head," my mother went on. "I don't want you to worry about it."

But on seeing Granny Pearl, there didn't seem to be anything to worry about, not until we got out on the porch after eating and she was suddenly talking about the fact of dying, talking and dragging us into it.

Once we were all gathered at the picket fence, she started in again. "I know what they're doing in there," she said, glancing at each of us in turn to see that we were all tuned in. "They're in there with Dewey Whittle tending to my business, which they think is soon going to be their business. That's what this gathering's about. It's not Christmas, is it? It's not Thanksgiving or Easter? So why else did the bunch of them come here all at once?"

It occurred to us only vaguely that she was castigating our parents, who by now seemed to occupy some realm far removed and less important than they were when we were all back home in our cities. Granny Pearl wiped her lips with a small handkerchief extracted from a big patch pocket in her dress.

"Last week, they took a picture of my brain," she said. "Did you know doctors can take a picture of your brain?"

"They can X-ray your bones," Lucas said.

"They don't call this X-ray," Granny Pearl said. "It's some other thing. They roll you into a tube. Once I was in there, a bell went off and I started thinking that this is what it must be like in the grave, lying alone in the dark, unable to move, only with dirt and earth worms all around. The doctor showed me a picture of my brain cut in half and a spot there that looked like a tiny gulf oyster out of its shell. That's what interested the doctor and what he said we had to worry about."

Grasping Juliette and Ezra by their hands, Granny Pearl turned and started on down the road. The rest of us followed, trailing along in a tight formation not to miss the next thing she had to say. Her stories were too good to miss and they stuck with you, especially the ones about New Orleans, where she grew up.

For example, she told us about an old, stooped woman, a fortune teller, who had a pet crow that thought it was dog. She said it barked in a dog-like way and had dog friends and pecked on steak bones and chased cats and squirrels around their neighborhood. And she said there was a raccoon that swallowed its own tail and strangled to death. Another time, she told us about a playmate of hers who, rummaging in a garden shed, got bit by a brown spider. Her bottom lip rotted and fell off.

These are the sorts of things Granny Pearl told us as secrets when we were free of our parents and what's more, you could never tell when she'd have something to teach us. For instance, how to make chewing gum from the sap she'd dig out of a sweet gum tree with a pocketknife she often carried, or how you could imagine something and dwell on it with your eyes closed for a long while and it would come to pass for real or else in your dreams, which, she claimed, was almost the same thing.

And she had a hundred riddles: *What flies all through the woods and never moves? And what invention allows you to see through a wall?*

We weren't fifty yards down the road when she shooed us back into the weeds to let a car pass. Once the dust settled and we had all waved—she had taught us to always wave because that's what neighbors did—we followed her eyes back toward the house. It stood old and solid under stacks of pure white clouds reflecting the sun— three stories counting the small attic windows, two gables, and a metal roof with its greenish patina—the house our grandfather Beale built is what we'd been told.

Granny Pearl shaded her eyes and pointed at the attic window in the far gable. She was up there in the middle of the night not long ago.

"Sleepwalking," she said. "I have taught myself to sleepwalk to take my mind off headaches. Nobody knows this and don't ever tell a soul. Especially your parents, do you hear me, Lucas?"

"Why not?" Lucas was large all over, a thick neck and a little slow-minded, if truth be told. Sweat was beaded on his forehead.

"Because right now they are back there cooking up a conspiracy," she said. "There's things you don't know about your parents." She stopped and looked us over. "I've got something new to show you all at the creek," she said.

Normally, Granny Pearl's mind hopped and skipped from one thing to another, but today, she seemed possessed of a single-mindedness directed at the grown-ups and whatever they were talking about. As we started down the road again, she circled back to the attic and said that last night she had sleepwalked through the pitch black up the stairs to one of the small windows. Outside, there was no moon or stars, but a glow floated over the surface of the earth and before long, it looked like it had been snowing.

"But remember it's October," she said, speaking directly at me. "Did you ever know of snow in the middle of an October night?"

"It's impossible," I said.

"Frank's right. It wasn't snow," Granny Pearl said. "It was cotton."

She said it used to be that the field in front of the house was planted in cotton. And when the cotton was high, it looked like snow piled up as far as a person could see. That night, there was a man coming through that snow. She said the man was dressed in rags and wore a felt hat like men used to wear when she was a girl. After a while, he slipped his hat off and waved it up at her. He called out, *come on, come on, it is time to leave this world. I've come for you.* "A man I would swear I never laid eyes on, though I was sure I recognized him and supposed I must have known him when I was a girl in New Orleans or else in a dream."

With that picture in our heads, we passed the small rock house with a side yard full of chickens and guineas. The neighbor's dog came out, a large black, bony dog with red-rimmed eyes named Shirley, who seemed to love Granny Pearl as much as we did. She romped, weaving in and out among the six of us and then, wagging her tail, licked Granny Pearl's dusty, bare feet, which appeared as hard and crusty as a pair of hooves, and fell in with us.

Shirley loved splashing and wallowing in the creek, which Granny Pearl called No Man's Creek, and knew we were on the way there because it was a place we often lingered when we went this way.

The road descended into a hollow filled with shade trees and then flattened out and crossed a one-lane wooden bridge so old it sagged in the middle so that even on foot you'd think it might give way. We stood with Granny Pearl on the bridge and looked at the creek water, clear and shallow here and running at a good pace over waving green grass until it turned downstream under a bunch of weeping willows.

Shirley was already in the water. The next thing we knew, Granny Pearl was down there with her. "Come ahead," she called out to us, "I'm going to the surprise." She turned and started downstream. Watching her moving along in the slow current with the hem of her dress floating around her, it seemed as if she was walking on water… or else pushed along by something other than her feet.

We all believed it, yelled and laughed and followed her, tripping along the bank through the huddle of weeping willows to a narrow sandy beach where she was waiting. The beach was covered with smooth, colorful stones, so many of them smooth and shiny in the sunlight and begging to be picked up. Coming out of the water, Granny Pearl retrieved a flat, blue one, drew her arm back, took a funny little jump, and threw it to hit the surface of the creek, skip once, and then disappear.

She plucked another one from the sand and commanded each of us to choose one, too, one that was smooth and flat and fit snug in our hands. There was a rush of happiness. We started practicing, the older ones helping the young ones. I teamed up with little Lisa, Charlene with Juliette, Lucas with Ezra. Again and again, we chose a pretty stone and threw with all our might at the surface of the creek, sometimes getting a skip. Lucas, who threw with a lot of force, got three skips more than once. How long we threw, I can't say; time skipped away like it had nothing to do with us.

Now back in the creek, Granny Pearl raised her hands in the air.

"You all listen," she called. "You all see this spot right here. This is my spot. This is where I want to be poured. Once I die, you all get together, bring the jar with the ashes in it, and pour them right here in these ripples."

Of course, at that moment, none of us could clearly fathom what she was talking about, "her ashes poured" being a foreign idea. But she went on to tell us that this creek, No Man's Creek, flowed into the

Thom Ball Creek and Thom Ball Creek into the Angelina River and the Angelina River into the big Neches and, if some fish or gator hadn't swallowed her up by then, part of her would wash into the Gulf of Mexico. In that warm saltwater was where she wanted to rest, she said.

Right then, against my will, I heard my father's voice—*she's lost a lot*—and I pictured a small oyster living in her head. She glanced at me like she had heard my thoughts but said nothing more and was undeterred. Reached into her big patch pocket, pulled out a cloth sack, and then another one. Told us to start filling them with stones, the prettiest, the best for throwing.

Of course, we did, joyfully choosing the ones that seemed to want to be thrown and soon the bags were full. Lucas took one bag and me the other and we started back upstream and were soon on the road again.

"Let's hurry, everybody," Granny Pearl charged us, heading out with water dripping from the hem of her muddy dress, and we formed ranks and fell in behind her.

Little Lisa, who had a round face and pixie hair just as a Lisa should, grabbed my hand. Juliette snuggled next to Charlene, who wore pink trousers and white shoes, and had great posture, both of them, I'm sure, terrorized by the thought of Granny Pearl becoming a smudge of dark ashes floating down No Man's Creek. Ezra, skinny with a pug nose, picked up a stick and started parading it as a sword, hoping for an angry rabbit or lizard or snake he could decapitate and save us from. Lucas lumbered along, his long Frankenstein arms dangling.

All the while, Granny Pearl contemplated whatever plan was in her head.

"What's conspiracy?" Little Lisa asked softly, squeezing my hand.

"It's like something that can fool you," I told her as Shirley, wet and muddy, shot past us, her tongue hanging out, her nose raking the ground, as if stalking ghosts, who tricked her into the briers and brambles and out again.

At a shout from Granny Pearl, Shirley suddenly angled left and plunged off the road into the thickets. We all stopped, looking around at each other. It was against the rules, our parents' rules, to ever venture into the woods and thickets where, they claimed, a person could soon be lost and fall prey to all sorts of miserable outcomes.

Nevertheless, Granny Pearl was fast disappearing, as if into the mouth of a green monster, expecting her troops to follow. Swinging his stick, a machete now, Ezra broke away and charged in. Lucas followed and then the rest of us close behind in single file. Thinking of snakes, I picked up little Lisa and pushed on through the head-high brush and bush and brambles, which tore at hands and arms and the girls' hair. In a few minutes, we were through the worst of it and on a sort of path. "Indian trail," Granny Pearl turned around and declared, cranking up our imaginations.

The path soon opened up and we were passing under big, shaggy trees, catching our breath, checking our body scratches. We skirted the banks of a slough half covered with green slime and then a line of turtles observing us from a floating log. In a muddy spot, the paw and claw prints of a creature probably a lot less fierce than we pretended.

At last, Granny Pearl led us into a clearing where Shirley was waiting stretched out in the sun. Nearby was an old well, long abandoned and covered with rotting planks that seemed woven together with spider webs. Granny Pearl called for Lucas and me to drag the planks off and without a word about danger or being careful—in other words, trusting us the way parents never would—she urged us all to drop to our hands and knees and crawl up to the edge of the well and peer in, which, without hesitation, we did. First off, you could hear the drip of water and feel the cool, earthy dampness rising up from the dark shaft into your face. There was the scent of loam and marsh mud and the sense of looking down into a forbidden world.

"My god, it keeps on going," one of us said.

"How deep is it?" Charlene asked.

"What's down there?" Juliette blurted out.

Shirley roamed around excited, as if she was expecting something fierce or ghoulish to emerge from the hole.

I lifted my eyes and noticed bloody scratches on Granny Pearl's feet and ankles as she dropped down to show us how to hang our heads out over the shaft, breathe in the musty dampness, and squeeze shut our eyes while dwelling on what was behind our eyelids. After a long, black meditation, we heard her whisper in a wavering voice, "careful now, open up and look straight down till you can see a face looking up at you." Juliette whimpered like a puppy. We could all feel a dread and hypnotic pull. In a minute, Charlene, who would grow up to be a beauty and liked center stage, released a breath: "I can see it. Oh, my God." Her voice expanded and then she said she could see a face floating in the air down there, water or something dripping off it, a round face, like a white moon, bluish eyes and an open mouth. "That's it!" Granny Pearl exclaimed and it wasn't long until we were all seeing the picture Charlene's watercolor words had painted. "A big open mouth," Ezra exclaimed, speaking for all of us. And without doubt, we were seeing something we weren't born to see and only Granny Pearl would be able to explain.

Granny Pearl told Lucas to take a stone from his bag and drop it straight down. We watched it flutter into the darkness and disappear. Then, a tiny chuckle as it plunged into water.

"You all see that face disappear?" Granny Pearl exclaimed and we nodded or said yes, it had crumbled away or popped or simply wasn't there anymore.

"What was it?"

"A haunt, angel or demon, nobody knows," she said, "but I can tell you what it's like." She said it was like a person buried in the pitch blackness of a grave and trying to get out through a hole in the earth. Only, the earth pulls back until the person is again surrounded by mud and dirt pressing in on them. And there's no room even to turn over.

We had never seen Granny Pearl scared before, but her voice seemed to shiver. She turned her eyes on Juliette. "That is what a plot is," she said to her, finally answering the question Juliette had posed back on the front porch and she said that's where those back at the house, the Parents, wanted to put her. They wanted to bury her in the Beale plot alongside that first woman Walter Beale married, the one who had all the children, and Walter Beale's crazy mother, who was there nearby, and the old man Beale, and others of those Beales and O'Harahs and Robertsons in the surrounding plots. People that had nothing to do with her.

There was a moment when a picture developed in our heads, all those creepy plots, especially the weird woman's who birthed all those children. "It's no fit place for me," Granny Pearl said in no uncertain terms.

Then, Shirley began to run a wide circle, barking and cutting up. Bathed in mystery and excited, we jumped to our feet and were off again—Ezra out front, confronting imagined enemies; Granny Pearl, our general, next; the rest of us soldiers falling in. Leaving the well behind, we crossed out of the clearing into a once plowed field grown up in tall weeds and patches of cottony thistles and, as we soon discovered, infested with yellow-green, big-headed grasshoppers. Screeching and screaming like grasshoppers weren't supposed to, they shot from the undergrowth like bullets aimed at our legs and chests, our hair and faces, and wherever they struck, their tacky feet stuck to us.

Up ahead, Shirley tore through the battlefield, a dark flash, crushing grasshoppers with her teeth. Charlene and Juliette turned in tormented circles, their long hair collecting them. Ezra was swinging his sword at the onslaught for real now and Lucas and me were flailing our arms, slapping, which did no good at all.

Granny Pearl called out above the racket to *line up! line up!* and follow her and soon she and Charlene were moving along with their arms stretched out like scarecrows, their heads thrown back and the grasshoppers collecting pretty as you please on their outstretched arms and hands but in a much less frenzied disposition. I lined Lisa and Juliette up behind me and we formed our own platoon and followed the path Charlene and Granny Pearl, in their bravery, were clearing for us.

What had been a scary and, in our minds, dangerous ambush soon became a joyous romp as our enemies had been defeated and we passed out of the infested weeds into the woods again. Once under the trees, which were dangling banners of Spanish moss, we started celebrating, hugging each other and dancing in the fallen leaves, as if we had won a battle.

Pretty soon, we found our bearings and took up a kind of march and we began to chant and stomp, providing a cadence: *Dirt or smoke, dirt or smoke, dirt or smoke…tied to the earth or rising to heaven….* It was a performance for ourselves and the sparrows and doves leaving the trees and Granny Peal. In essence, we had devolved into an army, our sensibilities sharpened to a fine edge, our minds filled up until there wasn't room for anything else. And we kept it up, more or less in rhythm, until the wild woods seemed to pick it up and vibrate, surrounding us with a sort of dazed light.

Passing out of the trees, we saw the barn far ahead and the pointed roof of the big house beyond it and realized that Granny Pearl had led us in a broad circle. Holding the dangerous wire for each other, we crawled through an old, sagging barbed-wire fence and came up straggling along until we finally reached the barn and then tromped around it to enter the broad open doorway, leaving the daylight behind and passing into a web of cool shadows.

We were a weary, ragtag army by then. Granny Pearl had Lucas and me get water from the tap out in front of the barn. We hauled it in an old, dented bucket, the water rusty colored with floating debris. Shirley got the first drink, lapping and splashing, and then the rest of us; nobody complained of the gritty, metallic taste, not even Juliette or Charlene, as we tilted the bucket, drowning our faces in it, lapping, slurping, each trying to outdo the one before and Shirley as well.

The crest of the afternoon was long behind us. The barn had fallen silent. It was near time to say our goodbyes, split up, and start the long drives home in the dark and lonely backseats of our parents' cars, where we would no longer be our true selves.

Then suddenly grimacing, Granny Pearl dropped her face into her hands. Her shoulders shook. "Oh, my head, my headache's coming," she called out through her swollen claws, which shocked and wounded us because we had had no idea or warning she was suffering.

We waited. After silent prayers, she looked up, calmer now, content it seemed, her eyes squinting and a tear dragging down her cheek, while each of us cursed the sick oyster in Granny's head. Then back to herself, she summoned Lucas and me, telling us to tote our sacks of stones up the ladder into the loft. Roused again, the others clambered up the ladder behind us and crowded round as we tumped out two piles of stones, pearly white, reddish-pink, blue and black and gray, some dappled, some veined and patterned. Following Granny Pearl's instructions, we divided them up, each one making a pile of the stones that fit into their fists, just as we had at the creek. Looking up from the floor of the barn, Granny Pearl stationed us a few feet apart.

We watched as she loosened her hair, spun it back into a tighter knot, thrust the wooden pin in place, and patted it smooth. She clapped her hands to get our attention. Shirley plopped on her haunches beside her, gazing up as if conducting an inspection.

"I'll be going for the others now," Granny Pearl announced.

She exhorted each of us to grip a stone, squeeze our eyes shut, and dwell with all our might on what we held in our fists. By the time they all get here, you'll know what to do, she told us then. And so, in our collective darkness, we imagined her leaving and waited, growing a little dizzy with energy and the height we commanded beneath rafters above the dirt floor of the barn. And in this strange liminal space, time lost its meaning and all together we had no doubt what a good soldier had a duty to do.

After a little while, our ears picked up a rumbling that evolved into a chattering, clucking, bleating, and you'd swear farm animals were coming back from the past. I peeked then and here came Granny Pearl and Shirley herding them, all six parents and Mr. Whittle, out of the sunlight into the barn. It took a moment for them to notice us in the loft above them and you could see an amusement spread over their upturned faces as if waiting for a performance.

There was my father's bald spot, more prominent than I'd ever seen it, my mother's short, bleached hair and hooped earrings. Uncle Claude's blistered face, Aunt Francine's head thrown back, revealing a knobby throat. From that high perch, one offering a vantage we'd never experienced, they were all at once strangely small, pack-like, one nearly indistinguishable from the other and, of course, ignorant of the pledge, the touch of magic, that held us together.

"What's going on up there?" Ezra and Lisa's mother, the biggest blob of all, said to no one in particular. Mr. Whittle, the old banker, pushed in front of the group of them, gazing up as if seeing us for the first time and a little dismayed. Granny Pearl stood with Shirley at the doorway in a bar of sunlight. She raised an arm and then, as she swung the double doors shut, the barn grew slowly dim and, in shadows, we began to understand what we were assigned to do.

A screech went up, "okay, enough, all of you. Get down from there!" One of them stabbed a finger in the air and soon they were milling around, mumbling among themselves. Ezra, the swordsman, stepped forward and launched the first stone and then Charlene and then Ezra again—and immediately we were all at it, releasing a flock of stones, darting, fluttering, sailing, something like the grasshopper attack. And I saw my stone strike and others bounce off shoulders, heads, startled faces, outstretched hands. There were gasps and squeals, loops of confusion, old Whittle hopping around like he'd stepped on a snake. Shirley began to romp and bark. And we kept throwing, emotions rising out of one mind, but not mindful enough to wonder what had happened to Granny Pearl or what was going to happen when the stoning was done.

Rosalina

They were married two years out of high school, two kids from small towns situated down the road from each other in southeast Texas not far from the Gulf Coast, a part of the world patched together by swamps and bayous and deep thickets. It was 1972 and once again, people were saying that the war in Vietnam was winding down. The groom, Robert Wilks, had drawn a high number and it looked as if he was going to be one of the lucky ones who beat the draft. Christine knew all about such things because the boy she was first going to marry was one of those who had come home from the war to a military funeral, all the town turning out for it.

When the wedding was announced, some said that Robert was getting Christine on the rebound, which was something she didn't try to hide from herself. She had promised to wait for Hayden Elliott and meant it, certain in her heart that if she believed he was coming home and made plans for it, he surely would. Her mind didn't allow her imagination to accept anything else.

When Robert first phoned and asked Christine out, she was still too distraught to respond. A few weeks later, at the downtown café with a friend of hers from high school, he came to their booth and, uninvited, sat down across from her, and then after an awkward beginning, apologized for calling her out of the blue. He had an earnest smile and, once he started talking, a steadiness in his brown eyes she had never noticed before. When she and her girlfriend went to the counter for their bill, he had already paid it.

A week later, he phoned again and sometime after that, they met at that same café on the town square. He mentioned Hayden, how much he had been respected by everybody. All of that and Robert's persistence, which she took for strength, was an unexpected comfort to the anger and anguish that had set her life back. When Christine's parents heard about Robert, her mother argued that it wouldn't hurt to let herself have some fun, pointing out that he was a good-looking boy from a Christian family and could probably go out with any number of girls if he wanted to.

For weeks, Christine had been pouring herself into thoughtless activities, painting her old bedroom, redecorating it so there was little left of her high school days, her days with Hayden. Then, with her mother's sewing machine, she started making skirts, blouses, fancy little jackets for her older sister and friends. When a cousin got pregnant, she found herself sewing baby clothes and, totally taken with it, was soon displaying a few of them for sale at the Saturday market on the square and donating others to the church pantry. She enjoyed thinking of people wearing her clothes and attracting attention. *Maybe I'll be a seamstress*, she told herself. She liked the old-fashioned sound of the word, the independence it might afford.

She and Robert, who had a good job with a pipeline company, started going out and on their third date, Robert talked about the scrapes he had gotten into in high school, running with a rowdy bunch of boys, drinking, and the serious trouble that had come from growing a patch of marijuana deep in the thickets. They were on the way to a movie in Beaumont. "I was lucky not to go to jail for it," he told her, "and might've without my dad knowing the right people and hiring a good lawyer."

Christine said she heard about it. "Just about everybody heard about it," she said, recalling the rumors, "but I never connected it to you."

"Dumb," Robert told her, "stupid." But he said he had grown out of that stuff and came to realize that, looking ahead, all he really wanted was what his dad had, a family and a nice house, maybe a big one, on a piece of land. A good wife, he went on, glancing at her from behind the steering wheel.

Sitting in bed that night with a book in her lap, Christine found herself considering those words Robert had spoken with assurance and honesty in his voice. With little effort or judgement, a future she had not considered before worked its way into her mind. She might never love another man, even a husband, in the way she ought to, but she could surely find a life satisfying enough to make up for it. There would be that and, also, she would turn herself into a seamstress, learn to design her own patterns, and open a small store with real customers. Without going too deeply into it, there seemed to be nothing more that she could be sure of or would ever want.

When the time came, they made a handsome couple, Christine with striking rust-brown hair that took on a reddish tint in the sunlight, a long, pretty face and olive skin, or so a Revlon lady had once told her. Robert, stocky and strong through the shoulders, black, longish hair, and a smile that helped a person believe whatever he said.

They rented a house that belonged to one of Robert's uncles and, with occasional help from friends, went to work on the place, laying new linoleum in the kitchen and bathroom, repairing swollen sashes, replacing fixtures, caulking and painting inside and out. The work was a new kind of healing for Christine, as well as a sealing of their relationship.

Once it was all done, the day the last paintbrush was washed and tools returned and put away, Christine, whose mood had lightened considerably, took Robert's arm. They stood in front of the small house happier than they had been and, in her mind, closer. She told Robert that now, while they could, they ought to take a real honeymoon, more than just a weekend, which is what they had settled for earlier.

Christine had an aunt she had long admired, her Aunt Jacquelyn, who lived in a small town on the Rio Grande River far on the other side of Texas, beautiful, idyllic country by the descriptions and pictures she sent Christine's mother. For a long time, Christine had had it in her head to go there and what's more, she exclaimed, she had planned to go on a Greyhound bus. "On a bus, we can just sit there without worrying about driving and watch the sights go by and we might meet interesting people, travelers."

Robert said that to him the bus idea sounded a little absurd.

"Well, that makes me want to go more than ever," Christine laughed.

They caught the bus before dawn in downtown Beaumont and it was a long trip over the interstate to Houston and then finally San Antonio where they changed buses for a second time and headed southwest. This was country neither of them had ever seen, vast stretches of flat, parched land, eroded gullies, scrub trees, and cactus to the horizon. The sun and sky dominant and hardly any bridges because there was no need of them. Many of the passengers now were Hispanic, men in straw western hats, girls with glistening, braided hair, old women in long cotton skirts, some who carried their possessions in knotted cloth bags.

In awe of it all, Christine wondered about the people and kept her eyes pressed against the window, absorbing the changing landscape. Robert dozed a lot. At one point, he moved close and looked past her. "I never saw so much of nothing," he said.

Two more times they changed buses and when they finally arrived in the small town that was their destination, dawn was coming up in shades of pink and red over the red earth and hills in the distance. They were still a long way from the river. A man named Guy, a skinny, snaggle-toothed man with a sparse gray beard and thermos of coffee, was waiting there for them.

The place he drove them to was hardly more than a settlement and tourist stop. It consisted of an old-fashioned general store that Aunt Jacquelyn ran, a couple of curio shops and campgrounds, a motel, and a bunch of adobe houses and trailers. Aunt Jacquelyn greeted them with hugs and a big breakfast in a kitchen in the back of the store. Christine hadn't seen her in several years, didn't remember how tall and thin she was, her skin sunbaked and rich with wrinkles, long, silver-gray hair trailing down her back. Christine's mother loved and admired her older sister, but the men in the family hadn't much good to say. Oddball, self-centered, independent, are complaints Christine had heard from them, as if her years of travel and refusal to remarry after the first one was a disgrace to womanhood.

It turned out that Guy, who was Aunt Jacquelyn's boyfriend, rented canoes. He would outfit people so they could paddle down river for a few days, camping along the way, and then he would meet them at a certain point and bring them back in his truck.

That's what Christine decided they had to do and by this time, Robert had accepted the proposition that when Christine got it in her head to do something, he might as well go along with it. In the early morning on the third day of their visit, in a green canoe loaded with supplies for a night and two days, they set out, the two of them, looking back at Guy and Aunt Jacquelyn's tall, thin figure on the bank, waving them on.

It was rough, solitary country on both sides of the river, American side, Mexican side. Guy had warned that once they got started, there wasn't any way out except at the pick-up point marked on a map full of landmarks, laminated and folded among their supplies. There would be a metal sign and red flag on the bank. "You can't miss it if you watch the map," he said. Pretty soon, they were caught up in this new, rugged world, varieties of cactus and bush and spiky desert plants they had never seen except in pictures on the banks and climbing the hillsides. In some spots, groves of prickly pear bloomed orange and yellow. Unlike the rivers and creeks they were used to, the water was cool, nearly cold, and moved along at a graceful pace, so paddling was easy and they were in no hurry anyway.

Late in the afternoon, they went through a series of rapids where they stopped and walked the canoe near the bank. An hour later, they passed into a canyon with high stone walls shading the river. Overhead, the sky was a narrow blue strip and buzzards rode the winds down into the canyon, disappearing and reappearing beyond one rock formation or another.

"I never thought it would be anything like this," Christine said, obsessed with it all, the ancient landscape, the rich solitude she felt. The pure desert air. She and Robert wore wide-brimmed straw hats Aunt Jacquelyn had given them and Christine had tied a bandana around her neck. As they approached a second canyon, Robert told her to lie back and let him paddle. And for a while she did, gazing up to watch the sky slide by in a dazed silence magnified by the pure emptiness and immensity of it all.

Two hours or so beyond the canyons was the campsite, but the spot marked on the map and by two flags was rocky, with only a few small trees and dotted with prickly shrubs. After walking around in the sun for a while, they loaded what they had unloaded and went on and not far ahead on the Mexican side, the side they were told not to set foot on, there was a strip of white sandy shoreline and further back a cluster of low-branching trees. It was, in Christine's mind, too good to pass up and they put in and set up camp in the huddle of trees, and then stripped and hurried down to the river for a swim.

The water was not so silty as the rivers back home, but deep and cool enough to bring chill bumps. After a while, feeling an urgency she hadn't felt in a long time, Christine swam up to Robert and took his shoulders, floating out in front of him. "Thank you for doing this for me," she said, meaning the river, the whole trip. "Hold me."

But then, about the time they were coming together in the water, the soft sound of clanking bells disturbed the quiet. Pretty soon, a woman and a boy appeared, out of nowhere it seemed, coming down a ravine with a small herd of goats. At first, they paid hardly any mind to the lovers in the water but sat down on a flat boulder thirty or forty yards upstream, letting the goats roam free while the woman began working on a basket she was weaving.

The couple moved apart, waiting for them to leave, but before long, it looked as if the woman and boy were settled in for a while. It was easy to get the feeling they were from out of some unknown past and had long been part of the landscape. The woman wore a loose blouse and dusty-looking brown skirt, black hair falling forward into her lap as she worked on the basket. The boy, who could have been nine or ten, wore baggy trousers and cowboy boots, a white bandana around his head. He stood on the boulder throwing rocks at the water and then at a speckled lizard as big as a small dog sunning on the far bank.

Finally, Christine said, "Come on, they're not going to bite." She took Robert's hand and urged him on. As they came up out of the river, the woman turned her head away, like she just realized they were there.

Under the trees, Robert and Christine dried off and dressed. They set up a canvas pup tent and started getting ready to cook supper. It wasn't long until Robert realized that Christine was missing. He looked in the tent and then stepped out of the trees and there she was up river talking, or trying to talk, with the woman, who still sat on the boulder. At this distance, he couldn't hear words but watched as Christine gestured with her hands and the boy and woman responded to her. *If I had a camera, it would be a good picture*, Robert thought.

"I used some of my Spanish," Christine said brightly as she came strolling back. "I never used any Spanish, except in class, or talked to a Mexican, but she could understand some. Her name's Rosalina." Christine was excited.

"Look, we ought to stay clear of them," Robert told her. "We're not supposed to be here anyway. Not on this side." He said they ought to go back to the American side.

"What for?" Christine's voice rose a little.

"Goddamn, we're trespassing or something worse." Robert looked into her eyes. "You heard what your aunt said about Mexicans."

"She never said a thing bad about Mexicans."

"Her and Guy, too, they said we had to stay on our own side."

"My god, we're a thousand miles from nowhere. Nobody's going to care one way or another which side we're on."

Robert crossed his arms, looked down, and pawed the red dusty earth, as if burning some pent-up energy. He turned and glanced over toward the woman, who was among the goats now at the water's edge. Across the river, the big lizard was raised up, stretching its neck, snapping at whatever was in the air. Robert couldn't help but wonder if it was poisonous. He had always heard desert lizards were poisonous.

By this time, the sky had turned a deep, inky blue with pale fingers of orange reaching above the hills and fish were starting to jump. As Robert set up the cook stove, there came the sound of bells again and when he came out of the trees to look, the woman and boy were gone, disappeared. But on the boulder was the basket and before he knew what was happening, Christine was running over there across the uneven ground. She climbed up and grabbed the basket, and then without looking back, started up the ravine. Robert yelled out once and then started running toward her, but she kept going. *Stubborn... pig-headed.* That's what flooded his mind. "Damn, goddamn," he spit out the words. A moment later, it came to him that the Mexican woman had probably left the basket on purpose for Christine and that his wife would soon be coming back with it.

Tensed up, he poured his misgivings into chores. He lit the cook stove, opened a can of baked beans, and cut a ring of link sausages into even pieces for frying. As time passed, his anger slowly evolved into concern and then worry. He turned the burners off, covered the sausage with a towel, trotted over there, and looked up the ravine, but no one was in sight. In the sky, a few feeble stars had appeared.

There was a hunting knife with the gear. Robert hurried back, strung it on his belt, and was soon on his way up the ravine. If they had been at home in the woods, the thickets, he probably wouldn't have felt any real misgivings. Girls back home knew how to take care of themselves in the woods, the marsh and swamps. But this was a different sort of country. Thoughts of what he didn't know about it stirred in his head—wolves, mountain lions, rattlesnakes in the rocks. All kinds of desert things to be afraid of if you weren't aware of them. The words "thieves, gangs" fluttered in his head as well.

The ravine was deep in some places, rocky, steep climbing, then it would level out and split into two or three directions. He would try one trail, calling out for her, and go back to take another one. Shadows were becoming more pronounced. He ran out of breath and out of patience and was on the verge of panic when he came upon some goat droppings and pushed on, following them as fast as he could. Reaching the very top of the long climb, he found a footpath. It wound through stunted mesquite and skeletal cactus and a few minutes later, there on a bench under a poor, shaggy tree, was Christine, she and the Mexican woman.

Feeling more relief than anger, Robert stayed back, watching them. The woman was short, stocky and, he could see now, somewhat older than he had thought at first. In the dusky half-light, the two of them were leaning in, absorbed in what they were doing.

"Christine," he called out and then once more, louder.

She looked up and looked again, as if suddenly realizing who he was.

"Is everything all right?"

"I lost track of time," she said. "Look, come here. I'm learning how to weave. We're weaving a mat." He could see that now, their fingers working with reeds or grass, the deep shadow of the branches falling over them. For a time, they continued with it as if he wasn't there, Christine trying out some Spanish words and the woman, Rosalina, Robert suddenly recalled, snug next to her.

After a while, with whatever they were making only partly done, the two stood up and Christine told Robert to come on, they were going to go to her place.

"What do you mean?" Robert said, coming forward. He didn't like it.

"She invited us, come on."

"What for?" he said, but they were already leaving and, without finishing what he might have said and maybe regretted, he followed them.

It turned out to be a small, mudbrick house with a flat roof in a settlement of huts and small houses scattered haphazardly over the hilly landscape. In front of the house was a kind of patio covered by an arbor made of scrawny limbs and vines. From here, looking west, there was a long view across scrub plains to a line of low mountains, their outline lit by an orange and red band of light, as if somewhere beyond them there was a blazing fire. Robert had never seen such a sunset or one that didn't compete with a line of trees. He felt much as he had that afternoon when they passed through the canyon, that he was small and this world a lot bigger than it needed to be. When he turned back, Christine and the woman had gone into the house. At the doorway, he waited while the Mexican woman lit two oil lamps, hung one from a rafter, and carried the other, leading Christine into shadows at the back of the room.

It was all one single room with a loft over the back part of it, two windows in front in what seemed a kitchen area, and the floor was smooth and shiny hard-packed clay. Hardly had Robert taken this in when the boy in the white bandana came through the open doorway hauling a bucket of water, a gourd floating in it. Right behind the boy was an old man who was dark and lean with bent shoulders and a bushy, gray mustache. The bones in his face stood out in the lamplight. Without acknowledging Robert, the old man spoke to the boy and the boy set the bucket down, dipped a gourd of water, and offered it up.

But Robert's mind had settled on Christine and this Rosalina, now on their knees beside a bed, a cot raised a few inches off the floor. There was a figure on it, a woman, Robert was finally able to discern. She was covered by a blanket. In a minute, Christine came back and took his wrist with both of her hands. "If I understood right, I think it's her grandmother," Christine said, tightening her grip. "She's sick, got sick not long ago, I think, but I'm not exactly sure."

Lying in lamplight, the old woman was small under the thin blanket with a furrowed face and mass of iron-gray hair floating over a pillow.

"Well, what the hell," Robert whispered. He buried his nose near Christine's ear. "The thing is we need to go. We don't belong here."

At once, the boy came closer and held up the gourd. Robert said no, shook his head, but then Christine took it from the boy's hand. "*Gracias*," she said. "You're Ernesto, *sí*?" The boy smiled and then wiped his lips with the back of a hand. Christine drank and offered the water to Robert. "Here, you must be thirsty. It's good. It's cool," she said.

"I don't want any."

"Robert, please."

"I don't want it and we got no business here," he said. "We don't know a thing about them or what the hell's going on or what the old woman's got and I don't feel right about it."

Christine drank the gourd empty. "Nothing's going on," she said softly. "Settle down. It's her grandmother and he's Rosalina's son. And the man..." She glanced across the room. "He's probably her grandfather. Damn it, we're here and I want to know more about them. I want to know if there's something we can help with. Really, you can wait outside if you want to."

Robert breathed in hard and, as Christine turned away, ran the fingers of one hand through his thick hair. "Fuck it, leave," Robert whispered to the situation, but more than that, he wanted to keep an eye on his wife and for her to realize that he had the right to take care of such things, take care of her. At the same time, he was getting anxious about the old man, who seemed downright haughty. Now, he was helping the boy lift the bucket of water up onto a table. On a nearby counter was an iron stovetop with two burners hooked to a glass jar filled with liquid, kerosene to judge by the looks of it. There were shelves lined with filled jars and bowls and sacks of various sizes. Pans and dishes were stacked along with what seemed to be cactus pads and also a pile of corn that hadn't yet been shucked. On the far wall was the picture of a prayerful Mother Mary on a calendar and beside it a metal cross and another carved of wood. A kitchen, Robert thought, that was out of a time he knew nothing about.

The old man left out the door on unsteady legs and the boy followed and a moment later voices could be heard outside. Two women dressed in embroidered blouses and baggy, white pants came through the door carrying baskets and behind them two men in cowboy hats and then kids, a girl and two youngsters. The two women didn't seem at all surprised to see Robert here. One of them spoke a few words to him in Spanish and the other one, who had ribbons woven into a long braid down her back, took a quick, shy glance into his eyes. They put the baskets on the counter and went to where Christine and Rosalina sat on the floor beside the cot. All at once, the hut seemed crowded, shadows climbed the walls and an earthy scent settled over the place.

It's gone on too long, Robert told himself. He was about to call to Christine, even drag her out of here if he had to, when she stood up and came over. "They want the men and children to go outside," she said.

"Outside? It's past time for us to leave," Robert said in a hushed voice. "It's getting dark, we don't even have a flashlight."

"Right now, the men are going outside," Christine said, "and Rosalina wants you to go with them."

"Chris, what the hell's in your head. We've got to go all the way back to the river in the dark, cook a meal, and get an early start. We're on a schedule here."

No answer, but the look in Christine's eyes, a stern tenderness when he had expected a fight, unhinged him.

"I can't tell you how much this means to me right now," Christine said, placing a hand on his arm. "She's had a stroke of some kind is what I think. My mother's aunt had a stroke when I was starting high school and I spent time with her and know what it looks like. Her hand's in a fist like hers was and she can't raise her arm."

"Hell, they've got doctors, don't they?"

"I don't know, doesn't matter. Right now, I want to help, to be here."

"I don't get it."

"Maybe you don't, but don't cause a scene, hear."

Outside, night was coming down. There were bright stars and enough light to show the men, three of them now, gathered beside a pickup truck, smoking.

One of the men, the one he hadn't seen in the house, walked toward him. "America," he said.

"Yeah," Robert said.

"We work over there," he gestured toward the river, "on the ranch with the stock and other things." He was smiling, a short, stout man with a big face. He wore jeans, a billed cap.

He asked Robert's name. "Robert, good," he said. "Me, I'm Luca." He shook Robert's hand limply. "And you have the woman."

"My wife, she's inside."

"Come on, come with me," the man named Luca said, walking to the truck. He whistled and the children, suddenly excited, ran across the yard and piled into the truck bed along with the men.

"Come on," Luca said again. "You want to eat. I invite you."

Robert looked down and then into the distance, calculating what sort of offer this was, how much he could trust the guy. It was an old truck but shiny and there were the children to ease his misgivings. Anyway, Luca was holding the door now. Robert glanced at the lit windows of the house, hesitated, and then slid into the cab. It was clean, smelled something like pine smoke. A crucifix and two feathers hung from the mirror.

They went down a rough, sloping trail, the truck rocking a little, headlights bouncing over the landscape and illuminating goats and cattle here and there. The road flattened and they entered a clump of trees where the old man, Rosalina's grandfather, was tending a fire in a stone-lined pit that had already burned down to a bed of coals.

Under a tarp in the back of the truck was a carcass, a goat Robert figured, but when the men strung it up on a limb, it was a small deer already gutted. As one of the men began skinning it, Robert suddenly reached the knife from his belt and came forward. "Let me," he said, to let them know he knew what he was doing.

In the firelight, he helped cut the ring around the deer's neck and then, working together, the two of them skinned it down—the shoulders, forelegs, and then the rest. There wasn't much fat and the little buck easily gave up its coat.

"You know the deer," Luca said as Robert was working.

"My family hunts," Robert told him. "I been hunting all my life, but they're bigger than this one where I come from."

The deer hung naked in the firelight. The meat was sliced off in strips and placed on a grill, then the ribs, the liver, the heart, and the tongue went on as well. The old man sprinkled salt, sparking sharp blue flames. As the meat sizzled and smoke blackened, he tended it with a long fork. After a while, the children moved close to the fire, begging until the old man passed out bites. The men looked on, smoking, talking quietly, drinking from a jar that was being passed hand to hand.

"It's made of the cactus, the fruit," Luca told Robert. "We make good alcohol like that many years."

The glow of the coals reflected in the milky liquid. When the jar reached Robert, he held it to his nose. The scent was slightly sour and the thought of drinking it after being passed mouth to mouth was more than he could manage. "Sorry, I don't drink," he said to Luca.

"You don't drink nothing?" Luca said, making a joke.

Robert handed him the jar. "I mean, I'm not thirsty."

Half an hour later, with the bones tossed in a ravine for dogs that had been moving about in the shadows, whining and waiting, and the meat packed in the back of the truck, they left together, the men, including Robert, hiking uphill while Luca and the children rode in the truck ahead of them. When they reached the house, the women were inside working in the kitchen, Christine among them. The place was brighter, candles flickering here and there.

In a moment, Christine came over, leading the woman, Rosalina, by the arm. Christine looked happy, a soft smile and her eyes bright. "We're friends already," Christine told him.

Standing beside his wife, this Rosalina seemed to Robert more displaced than ever. In the flickering light, her hair shone as if oiled. She wore dangling earrings that seemed to be made of coins, the same as those on the other women. Her face was round and her nose broad. A thin scar ran from the corner of her mouth, suggesting a life more complicated than he could hope to imagine.

"I'm sorry about your mother, grandmother," Robert said, at last.

Rosalina glanced at Christine like she was waiting to know what the man had said. But Christine just pulled her closer. "We're going to eat in a minute," is what she told Robert. "They're making tortillas and beans and other things. I'm starving, aren't you?"

But he wasn't starving, just wrought up with impatience and fear of what Christine might have in her head. Despite the fine moments skinning the deer, he was determined to leave, nothing more. At last, though, he said, "Okay, but after we eat what they've got here, if we can eat it, we go. We go, no matter how dark it is."

"I heard you the first time," she let out abruptly and turned away.

The women and children ate inside, the men out under the stars, crouched near the dimmed headlights of the truck. The meat was charred, stringy, and wild. The beans folded inside thick, warm tortillas were delicious. There were peppers and something that seemed like strips of cactus. Before long, Robert chanced a drink from the jar the men continued to pass around. It was slightly tart and then fiery going down but warm in the stomach once the fire had passed, leaving, after a short time, a desire for another sip. And so he drank, passed the jar, and ate as his stomach allowed. Afterward, the men lingered outside the way men in his family would, segregated from the women after a big meal. Robert experienced an unexpected satisfaction in that, the satisfaction of a full stomach in the company of other men, even if he couldn't understand them and only guess at what they might be saying to each other or about him.

Though he hadn't smoked in a long time, a promise made to his mother when he graduated high school, he accepted a cigarette from Luca, who then lit it. Robert puffed on the heady tobacco, watched the crimson ash burn and, before long, began to drift away from the others until he was walking out beyond the truck lights into the night and in that leaving began to feel a great, unexpected relief at finally being alone and in control of his own wits again. It was chilly, this desert air, and his head was swimming a bit from the strong drink and in the midst of that discomfort, he recalled the words Christine had said to him earlier. *I heard you the first time*, is what she had said in a scolding voice, or at least that's how it struck now.

He looked out at the ocean stars, the brilliance of them, and immediately, as if in response to them, realized that he had left the campsite unattended, the boat, everything else could be gone when they got back. In the next breath, he recounted what it would take to follow the winding ravines back down in the dark, no idea which turn to take when a ravine branched, how vulnerable they would be to anything out there, the chance of falling, breaking something, of finally ending up lost or in a circumstance they couldn't escape from.

In short, all the practical things a husband had to consider and Christine, in her rush to have an adventure, never thought about. The truth being, he hadn't wanted to make this trip in the first place, endure all those hours on a Greyhound bus, meet Christine's long absent aunt, who she seemed so taken with, spend two days on a river he knew nothing about. All he ever wanted was to stay home, get started on their marriage, and get used to living their new life.

Turning back, he saw the truck lights dim and go out. When he reached the house, the men were gathered under the arbor and the women were inside. Two candles shown in one of the windows. They stay in, was Luca's explanation when Robert asked about the women, and Luca said the men would sleep out here.

"Why don't you all just go home?" It seemed crazy.

"This is what we do." Luca shrugged, placing a strong hand on Robert's shoulder.

After being given two thin, woven blankets, Robert bedded down with the other men on the hard earth under the vine-covered roof of the patio. Rosalina's boy and the other children slept in the bed of the truck. For a time, Robert felt the urge to go inside and confront his wife, see what she was up to, why she preferred to be in there with strange women in their strange world rather than out here with him, unable to acknowledge what his nature denied, that he was shot through with jealousy and dishonored by it.

For a long while, wrapped loosely in the blankets, Robert lay on his back brooding under the dead leaves and vines, his mind contemplating the creatures that might be up there waiting to drop down on him. Until, as if of its own accord, a deep weariness set in.

When he woke, Robert found himself alone in the chill of the morning. He wriggled out of the blankets and sat up, pulled his shoes on, and walked across the yard out into desert and peed, gazing at the far away hills that seemed more distant now that they were no longer on fire. Yet the sunlight was creeping across the land as if being controlled by a steady hand. Bees circled around nearby cactus blossoms. A long, brown and yellow snake hurried through the brittle weeds. When he got back to the house, Christine was outside waiting.

"Did you sleep?"

"Not a lot. Did you?"

"Actually, yes. There's some coffee inside."

"I don't want any coffee. We need to get going."

"Robert." She stepped back, looking at him. "Listen to me a minute." He waited.

"I've got something to tell you. Please don't get mad, but I want to stay for a little while."

"Stay? You mean here?" He looked straight at her. "No, you can't. You're not," he said.

"I don't mean for long, a couple days maybe."

"Days? What the hell you talking about? For one thing, what are you gonna eat?"

She smiled like it was a dumb question, like he was dumb. "What they eat," she responded softly. "It'll be for just a little while, two days."

"I've got a job, Chris. They didn't give me two more days. Besides, we're on a schedule, we got to meet him, Guy."

"When you get back, tell Aunt Jacquelyn where I am. She'll come for me if you can't."

"To hell with her."

"Or they'll take me back," Christine said. "They go across the river all the time."

Robert felt hot tears at the back of his eyes and a need to continue this until she came to her senses. He dug in, stringing out the argument in one direction and then another until Christine's face was flushed, her gaze growing harder. She stood in her dirty jeans and half-buttoned shirt like she was planted here.

"Luca said a doctor's coming. He speaks English and I know what questions to ask."

"What the hell," he said and spit to one side and, at last, knew it had played itself out. He went silent. Christine stepped up close, placed her hands on each of his arms and planted a brief kiss on his lips. "At least let me get you some water."

He didn't answer but turned away and started walking. A minute later, when he looked back, she was gone and there was nothing to see that he wanted to see.

At the river, he drank nearly an entire canteen of water and poured the last of it over his head. He began packing up, slowly at first and then suddenly with a fury, grabbing one thing after another, stuffing them haphazardly into bags and the canoe. He felt worn out, cheated. He glanced at his watch and then the sky, waded into the water, and eased over into the canoe. He put on the big straw hat against the harsh sunlight. He looked downriver to where it turned past a wall of cane and started out, his mind filled with a persistent thought—once they both were home and settled, he would sit her down and get things straight so their life would be the way it was supposed to be, had to be.

Brothers-in-Law

Foley Atwater, a man of fifty-seven and part of a big, close-knit family, understood what it meant to carry a coffin, comfort the grieving, stand in prayer over an open grave, but he never imagined he would find himself in an unforgiving place like this digging one.

They chose a spot near a big, bearded oak a hundred yards off a ruined logging road that lay somewhere between the Angelina Forest and Big Thicket Preserve—a landscape of river bottom, East Texas jungle, and black water sloughs. It was barely morning, the air damp and chilly, the small clearing freckled with dim sunlight falling on leaves, ty-vines, and strangled saplings. Foley walked a circle, stabbing the earth with a narrow-bladed spade, digging to test the soil, and then bringing up sodded leaf mold, bits of oak rot long-ago buried, and the smell of decay.

"That's God's compost," Mel said. Mel, his brother-in-law, stood a few steps back, holding on to a pick with a mattock blade.

Foley grunted. He wore a faded, long-sleeved cotton shirt and denim overalls, a stout man, half bald, with rounded shoulders, thick arms, and big hands, a blacksmith's hands.

The small clearing, as much as one could hope for in these thickets, was hemmed in by prickly shrub and wax leaf bush, the shadowy outline of willows not far away. The small body, such as it was, lay in a makeshift canvas bag shoved under a patch of shrub at the edge of a shallow pond. Mel had purchased the canvas and a curved upholstery needle at a hardware store and done the stitching himself using nylon fishing line.

Long before dawn, they had left their hometown in northeast Texas in Foley's GM pickup truck, the canvas bag wedged in the truck bed under fishing and camping gear in the unlikely chance they would be stopped on the road by some deputy or highway patrolman. A mostly silent trip it had been until out of Nacogdoches on U.S. 59, Mel leaned forward and switched on the radio—suddenly the loud, urgent voice of a preacher who seemed to be having a fit, and then *static,* and then a hillbilly song sung by a woman cut short by Foley's sharp voice.

"Damn it, turn it off."

Mel did.

"Sit still and do without noise for a while."

"Sorry," Mel said and sat back in the near dark to gaze across the long hood at the beams of the headlights gobbling up the highway. Then a minute later, Mel cocked his head.

"At least give me a clue how much further."

"A ways," Foley responded, moderating his temper. "Far enough that I'll be able to forget where it's at."

Mel took a breath. "Look, the worst is behind us. Under the circumstances…"

"You want me to turn around, Mel. You keep on talking and breathing like you're going to suffocate, I'll turn around and go back home. I'm getting a headache."

The circumstances, the story that was driving Foley's deep vexations, had come out of Mel's mouth the day before late in the afternoon. He showed up at Foley's metal works and welding shop just before closing time, fidgety, red-faced. At first, Foley thought he might be drunk by the way he looked, though Mel had never been much of a drinker. Foley sent him into his office at the back of the shop, left his employees to clean up, closed the office door, and poured what was left of the day's coffee into two dirty cups because coffee was a habit when he had a sit-down visitor.

Mel took his cup in two hands and sat down in a swivel chair, the knot of his tie nearly hidden by a roll of fat, his eyes staring down at the coffee one second and out of the barred glass window the next.

Foley propped his butt against the desktop, waiting. The smell from an arc welder hung in the air. Mel set the coffee aside and lifted a copy of the *Cobb County Register* from the patch pocket of his dress coat, opening it to the front-page headline and below it the picture of the eleven-year-old girl everybody was looking for, a girl named Leslie, Barrett her last name. She had gone missing two days before, a Tuesday, somewhere between the downtown city park and her home up on West Roseland Street a few blocks from there. Her father an executive at the new tire factory on the outskirts of town.

"I need to tell you something," Mel said. "It's been tearing me up all day and I'm confused about it, what to do." He glanced up at Foley's face, took a sip of the bitter coffee, and without holding back, started in.

"The fact, the fact is, I know where she's at," he uttered, his voice going solemn. Early that morning, before breakfast, he had found the girl, her body, in the hayshed at the back of his property. He said he was getting feed for the three goats that Ida was raising. Ida usually fed them, but this morning he decided to let her sleep in. Their little collie had gone with him and the second they entered the shed, the dog started throwing a fit, barking and pawing at a pile of hay back in one corner, and she uncovered the girl.

At first, Foley wasn't sure he was hearing what his ears were hearing, his mind having trouble catching up to Mel's words and the broken look in his eyes. "That girl there?" he asked, glancing at the picture.

"Yeah." Mel said. "I'm sure. She was dressed in shorts and a white shirt and baseball cap and barefoot. I recognized her from the paper and then, naturally, my first thought was to run to the house and tell Ida and report it to somebody. I started to, believe me, I wanted to. I meant to, but after a little while, I began thinking about Ida, how it was going to upset her, excite her. You know how she is."

"That don't make sense," Foley said.

Mel gave a little convulsive shake of his head. "I wanted to do the right thing, but then there's something else about it."

Foley waited.

"It's her mother, the girl's mother. I'm afraid if it came down to it, she might say she recognized me."

"Hold on a minute," Foley said. He set his cup down and stood up. He wiped a fist across his mouth, his heart running fast in his chest. His mouth was dry. He opened the office door and walked out into the shop to free his head of Mel's voice and let some of his agitation settle out. The shop was empty, quiet, the big overhead door in front of the building was open and pale sunlight poured in onto the concrete floor and racked supplies and machinery. He pushed the button and watched the screeching door go down as he had thousands of times before. He went back into the cramped office.

"Okay," he said, "tell me what you're talking about."

Swallowing something down his slack throat, Mel went on, telling him that every Saturday there was a girls' softball team that practiced in the park. He liked to take his sandwich down there and sit on the wall and watch them. One Saturday not long ago, after the game broke up, this one girl was left by herself waiting for her mother to pick her up. A tall girl, Mel said, the best player in the bunch. "Well, I went across the street to the Mini-Mart and bought a bazooka and came back and gave it to her. You know, ice cream in a paper tube."

"I know what a Bazooka is," Foley snapped.

"So, what the hell, her mother drove up and got out of the car. She wasn't happy about it, the ice cream. She was fit to be tied and loud and gave me a piece of her mind. That's all there was to it. After that, she drove off. I swear it."

"Goddammit, Mel."

"Foley, that's all there was to it. It's obvious what happened. Somebody was driving by on that dirt road, somebody in a big hurry. He saw my shed right by the road and dumped the body in there and covered it up to get rid of it. To leave somebody like me to take care of it."

"Why are you telling me this?"

"You know why. To get some support when the time comes."

"Look here," Foley said. "There's the phone. Pick it up. Call the police or, better yet, Sheriff Yarbrough. Tell him to meet you out there and get this thing straightened out."

"I can't. Listen, look at it this way. They always blame the one that finds the body. Everybody knows that. You know it." Mel pulled out a wadded handkerchief, wiped his damp eyes. "And then there's the mother and other mothers and girls. They are going to recognize me just for being there sometimes. Crap, think about it. It's all coincidence, but if I report it, the girl, I'm dragged into it. The next day, my name's going to be in the paper and if the law comes asking questions, I don't know how I could handle it, what they might make me say. The idea scares me. Think of Ida. How it's going to affect her mind. Think of the family. Mother Mary. Your brothers. All the rest. And there's the fact that Ida and me don't have any kids. People think that's not normal. I'm not normal. And I wasn't born here and people are always looking for a scandal, something to talk about. No matter how innocent I am, I could get the blame."

"What in God's name do you expect me to do?"

"Help me. You know how much you've always meant to Ida and me, Foley, people look up to you. What I'm thinking is you tell them on that afternoon, when the girl went missing, I mean, I was with you. We were doing something together, fixing a fence. If it was you talking, nobody would question it, not for a second."

Foley set his jaw.

"It's not really lying. It's telling a story so people won't believe a lie."

Foley entertained the urge to grab his brother-in-law by the neck. He didn't. He wanted to spit the sour out of his mouth. He didn't do that either. He was hungry. Supper would be waiting.

"I'm hungry," he said. "I'm going home to supper. To think."

"The longer we wait, the worse it's going to get."

"We? We? Get the hell out of my chair." Foley forced his tongue to slow down. "Go home and don't tell a soul we talked," he said. "Not Ida, especially. Nobody. I'll call you. After supper, I'll call you."

When Foley's sister married Melvin Combs, it was pretty much understood by the family, though unacknowledged, that he was as good a match as Ida, a fragile girl whose mind worked slower than most, was likely to make. Over time, it worked out. Mel had a silver tongue. He flattered the women in the family, Foley's aunts and in-laws, and finally, his mother, Mary, grew fond of him. Foley's two brothers tolerated him, helped to renovate an old farmhouse Mel and Ida had bought. Physically, he carried too much flesh on too little skeleton—not the steadiest post in the fence, Foley's father commented, speaking of his disposition as much as his body. But Mel was there to help when help was called for. He's the one who got the old man to the hospital when he suffered the first stroke. And after a few setbacks, which included a brush with the law over shady oil leases, made a plausible living selling furniture and carpet off the floor of the major furniture store in town.

At straight up six, Foley had supper with Sue Ann, his wife of nearly forty years, silently watching the local news and weather report while thoughts collected in the web of his mind: the mystery of Mel's simple story, Ida's nervous disposition, the shame to the family should his brother-in-law's name appear beside the girl's, the effect on his business, the lie Mel had asked him to tell, the girl and her family, which were, in fact, beyond help now. Foley had never been in fear of anything, not that he could recall or would admit to, and now here he was shivering in the face of his brother-in-law. There were no good answers where Mel was concerned and finally, in resignation, he settled on the quickest, most practical one, which is what he related to Mel when he called him at straight up seven beneath twinkling stars at the edge of his back pasture.

"Two things," Foley said. "I don't want to ever lay eyes on her, you hear. And I'm wary of your tongue. Don't let on to Ida, to anybody, that we're going to be together tomorrow. Say there's a cousin in the hospital in Texarkana or Shreveport or some other place you've got to visit. Or something. No, say that and stick to it."

Morning was fully born, warming up, the clearing shot through with patches of sunlight. Mel swung the mattock as best he could, breaking up the muck, tearing back buried vines and roots. Foley sat close by on his haunches, using a green stick to scrap muddy clay from the blade of the shovel. Despite all, he wanted to dig a proper grave— deep enough to keep razorbacks and bobcats and feral dogs or any other predators from getting into it. Already, though, Mel seemed half worn out, the digging more than his mind and body could tolerate.

"We might've picked an easier spot," Mel huffed, sweating.

"I told you to shush your mouth." Foley threw the stick aside and moved in with the spade. He had warned Mel to keep his voice down, fearing that some curious game warden or hunters could be wandering about. In the dark of early morning, turning onto the ruined logging road that led to a creek where Foley and his brothers used to camp, they had come upon a road kill, a possum probably, surrounded by turkey buzzards, stubborn creatures casting shadows in the headlights. One of them was pulling lose a long strand of bright red meat. It troubled him then that there might have been a vehicle on that road not long before.

After two feet or so, they had hit clay, orange and chalky at first, and further down dark and sodden, sticky. Mel had settled into a routine. He would take a turn with the mattock, swinging it like it weighed a ton, and then soon enough move aside to rest. He would stand there wavering until Foley climbed into the hole to spell him, and then, free of the labor, Mel would make his way over to the edge of the pond near where brambles took over, where the body was. Out beyond the pond, sprouting in marshy land, were stands of palmetto, bunching and spreading into the forest.

After two hours, his patience frayed and anxious to get done with it, Foley began using the mattock and the shovel, too. Water was seeping into the hole, a tiny trickle and then more. It softened the clay and clotted the dark earth some, making the digging easier but a mess to deal with.

Mel came out of the undergrowth. He was working his jaw on something. "Chinquapins," he said in a low voice, smiling. He leaned over, revealing a handful of the round nuts. "There's a tree over there beyond where she's at. When I was a kid, I used to love these things." He cracked one with his back teeth, squeezing his eyes shut.

Foley climbed out of the hole, trailing water. He held out the shovel. "Let's get this done."

He waited while Mel spit splinters of shell and then slowly pulled on his muddy gardening gloves and eased down into the deepening pit. There was a brackish odor. Swamp water. Foley stood over him like a prison guard, watching as Mel spaded water and then mud up onto the mound that was taking shape.

"You know something," Mel said, pausing to look up. "The picture didn't do her justice. She was a pretty girl, long, silky, reddish hair. You don't see it in the picture."

"What are you talking about?"

"Well, and she was wearing little gold earrings. Something the paper didn't mention."

"You mean you looked her over?"

"I had to be sure, didn't I?"

"What in God's name? Shit. Mel, your mind's damn twisted up."

"You can't say that."

"I said it," Foley said. "One minute we're working and the next you're…" He didn't finish his words.

Mel's face hardened. There was silence until finally, "my throat's dried out and the water's back in the truck. I'm about to drink this here."

Foley ignored him.

"It'd probably kill me, though."

Foley started walking away, a headache building, throbbing at a spot over his left temple. He eased down and settled against the fat trunk of the oak, laid his head back, and closed his burning eyes, wrestling with black thoughts, thoughts of his decision to toss his conscience aside and drive sixty purgatorial miles into the night. Trying to ignore the bitter clamor in his head, he glimpsed an armadillo emerging from out of the bush over near where the girl was. The animal started across the small patch of open ground and then stopped to poke its nose into the dead leaves, hunting bugs. Another followed and then a third, each one in turn unhurried, as peaceful, in their armor, as any creature on earth could hope to be.

All at once, Mel spoke up. "Foley, hey. How much more of this do we have to dig out? We're getting more water in here."

Foley crawled to his feet. In a second, he was standing at the edge of the pit. "Mel, I've asked you to keep your blasted voice down."

Mel was gazing at grubs, a dozen of them, floating in the mud-gray water. A yellow salamander swam through the muck and began climbing up out of the hole. "I got spiders in my stomach," Mel went on. "I'm shaking. I need to drink something." He threw the shovel and started climbing from the trench. "I'm going back to the truck for the water." He was soaked to the waist, his cheap nylon shirt splattered with mud and clay. The outline of his undershirt showed through.

"Not happening," Foley said. "I don't want you near the road or walking up on somebody who's going to ask questions." With the pick in hand, he slipped down into the pit. He struck through the water and looked up. "Wait over there. Sit against the tree and wait's all you have to do. I'll call when I'm done."

"I mean to do my share."

Foley gestured with the sharp point of the pick. "Shut your eyes, stretch out, and don't think or talk, for God's sake."

Half the morning was gone and still the grave was a long way from what he had set out to make it. Two feet down, the sides had begun to crumble in spots; the bottom under the water was too narrow. It was, in fact, little better than an ordinary hole any redneck kid could dig. He cussed it, he cussed himself. "Look here." Foley said, his voice straining. "Close your eyes. Be still. Stay out of trouble."

Foley massaged his temples and then got back to it. Cool sweat ran down into his collar and mosquitoes had found him, buzzing circles. Caught in the fact of his own vulnerability, the green canopy and vegetation pressing in, Foley was consumed by a creeping urge to get to what whispers in his head were arguing about—what acts his brother-in-law was truly capable of.

For a while, Mel sat in the shade of the tree, his head in his hands, as if he might be praying or sulking. Then, it got so quiet one could hear the breeze in the treetops. And Foley realized that Mel had disappeared. Gone to the truck is what he assumed, which fired his anger again. Except for trimming up some and getting more of the water out, he was ready to quit.

He began baling with the shovel and was soon getting ahead of the seepage. He paused to take a breath and, beyond the clearing, spotted Mel over there where lay the girl. He was on his knees leaning into the briars like some foreign supplicant before an altar. The urge struck Foley to yell out, shoo him away from there, but already there had been too much noise. He leaned on the handle of the shovel, watching.

Finally, he called, softly. "Mel, get away from there. Leave it be."

Walking toward the grave, Mel said, "I decided something. I've got to tell them about what happened with her mother at the park, to get ahead of it, in case it comes up at some point."

Foley said nothing.

"And like we said, you're going to vouch for me. And now, since we're here together, we have to vouch for each other. That's clear, isn't it."

Foley stopped work. He read the lines in Mel's face, realizing that his brother-in-law had come to his shop not just for help, but to trick him. And now here they were, in it together. Humiliation and a shot of infernal anger went through him.

"Look at me, Mel. Look. Now listen to what I'm asking you. Did you have anything to do with it?"

"What?"

"Did you harm the girl?"

Mel's head jerked up. "Hell no. No. How can you ask that?"

"Did you ever speak to her other than that one time?"

Mel said nothing. His tongue seemed to have dried up. He shook his head. Finally, he said, "No, sir."

"I'm thinking you did. Why else would you be so worried about her mother?"

Mel shook his head slowly and paused, like a kid searching for a lie.

"Was she ever in your car, Mel?"

"My car?" Mel turned his back to his brother-in-law. He faced out toward the thickets as if contemplating them and in a moment, took off, walking across the open ground into the mouth of the trees, the shadows.

Foley watched until he was convinced that Mel wasn't soon returning. He swore with a conviction that could have been an unholy prayer. He went back to work. Baling water again, licking at sweaty lips, his own thirst beyond anything he could remember experiencing.

For a while, except for the sound of the shovel, the splash of water, it was very quiet.

When Foley glanced up again, Mel was walking toward him with a jug of water he had retrieved from the cab of the truck. He turned it up and drank and then held it toward Foley. Foley didn't reach for it. He waited, waited for words to come out of Mel's mouth, and soon they did.

"It's not what you'd think," Mel said. "It's something outside of explaining, an accident, I swear, Foley. First, her mother was late coming for her. And the girl was aggravated about that. We talked a minute while I was in the car and I wasn't about to buy her ice cream again, but she said would I take her to her friend's house. She got in with her baseball bat and a glove, a first baseman's mitt. She got in because she wanted to. We sat a minute and to let her get comfortable. I asked her a riddle. You know I know a lot of jokes and riddles and the kids love to hear me tell them. She knew a few herself. We started trading them back and forth. I guess I forgot about the time, but now she wasn't in any hurry either. We drove around to the back of the park to get out of the sun. There's a riddle where you count on your fingers and after that, I took her hand to show her how to read palms. She got into it. We were having fun. Her hair's different, what I call corn silk hair. So when I thought about touching it, she didn't say no. It was innocent, but for some reason, all at once, she got upset. Her voice changed, the look on her face changed, which scared me. She started saying 'you touched me, you touched me…I wantta go home' and wouldn't stop."

Mel paused briefly, his eyes raked Foley's face. "She tried to get out of the car, but you can see, I couldn't let her in that state. I locked the doors with the latch on my door and that set her off in a tantrum. She poked the bat, hit me in the face, hard. It hurt. We started wrestling for the bat. So I was in more trouble. Bigger trouble. These days a girl can cause a grown man to go to jail, prison. Girls have a lot of power, Foley."

As Mel went on, Foley watched his face assume an expression that made him seem to age and grow old. His chin wrinkled. His eyes glistened. He clung to the jug of water, Foley's parched throat on fire.

After a sip, Mel said, "If her mother hadn't been late, nothing would have happened. If she hadn't wanted in the car. If there wasn't the bat. If she hadn't been taught like all of them to watch for bad men. Things got out of hand. God knows I like little girls, but there was something not right with her. Listen, you know I'm basically a person of loving kindness."

As Mel continued, water crept up Foley's legs, warm, filthy water seeping in as if from some ancient, buried swamp.

"Look here, I'm not going to condemn you," Foley said. "And I won't turn you over to the law. Give me a hand up out of here."

"You promise? Jesus, thank you."

"Give me a hand," Foley repeated.

"Talking helps," Mel said. "It makes me feel better to talk, but I've been thinking. I'm a deep thinker, Foley. People don't realize that. But this time I was too upset to think. She threatened me and kept on and wasn't going to stop until her sour mother knew about it. They're people of means that family and one word from her would crush me. What was I supposed to do? Look, I shut my mind and didn't know what else to do. I'm sorry, so sorry. I promise this, I'm going to be a better person, better man for Ida and the family. You'll see..."

"Damnit, shut up!" Foley broke in, shaking off Mel's ungodly peroration. "Now help me out of here."

Dropping the water jug, Mel sank his knees into the mud beside the grave. He reached out a hand and Foley latched onto what felt like soft, boneless flesh. He acquired a firm grip and yanked Mel headfirst into the pit, pressed a boot down on his back, and used the pick like an axe.

∼

It was 3:05 by the dashboard clock when Foley turned off the logging road onto the blacktop. There was nothing left of the possum carcass but a scattered skeleton and pile of dry fur. The grave in the thickets was properly stomped flat and hidden under dried leaves and spiky brush. The girl rode with him as she had that morning. He will take her back to a decent spot and place her on soft pine needles where she can be easily found. Where the family and town will claim her. In Foley's mind, a mind not used to self-reflection, he reflected and began to feel at ease and before long at peace with himself, believing that he had done what had to be done—for Ida, for his family, for the girl, for holy justice.

And he settled back on this mild, sunny Friday afternoon, watching the highway and wooded landscape go by. Crossed a long bridge over a stretch of swampy earth and then in a little while, his thoughts began to turn on himself and it seemed as if it wasn't yesterday but years ago that Mel, the damned buzzard, had come into his shop, sat down, and opened his mouth. And now Mel was out of the picture. He'd paid his price, while he, a man of fifty-seven, would be paying for the rest of his life.

Richard and the Wasp

A black wasp circles the man's upturned face, moving out of his line of sight and back again, its slender wings swiftly vibrating, or so it seems. Soon, as if satisfied with its reconnaissance, the wasp lands on the man's chin, makes its slow creeping way up a cheek, leaps onto his broad nose, and peers into his nut-brown eyes. Cross-eyed, because that's the only way he can take in the worrisome creature, the man peers back. Gently, his strained mind addresses the wasp...*you're welcome here for company. Lord knows I love good company. But don't sting, don't dare sting me, not in the face.*

Richard Plough is fifty-eight and larger than most in every direction. He wears rough work boots, a gray, woolen coat with red lining, and lies flat on his back on a carpet of autumn leaves beside a rotting log, unable to move. His legs, his hips, his arms, even his shoulders are numb, useless. An hour, maybe two, he has been lying here helpless like this, though it's impossible to know for sure since the clock in his head is out of whack. The thing he first accepted was that he had been shot in the stomach or maybe the chest or possibly the back by a hunter in a camouflage coat and billed hat. He knew this because the moment he heard the sudden report of a rifle, he had found himself lifted up and thrown off the log, where he had been sitting to rest and think for a while.

Along with the sound of the blast, a quick, sharp sensation, like needles of lightning, shot through his body and then, as if a switch had been thrown, nothing. No conscious connection to the earth or anything below his neck. Opening his eyes, his ears registered the rattle of dry leaves. Then the hunter appeared, but at a dim distance so that he was no more than a vague image mouthing something, possibly a question, but in a voice so shredded with echo Richard couldn't decipher the words. As the man came forward, Richard forced his eyes to close, locking out the light, a dead man now, the only defense his confused brain could imagine against a man with a gun. But then, if he wanted to ask for help or some such thing, he probably couldn't; his tongue seemed to be swollen, filling his mouth.

In a little while, there came another, much different voice, somewhat stronger than the first one, yet high-pitched, easier to make out. Assertive. A taking charge sort of voice. And Richard felt the presence of a new pair of eyes trying to drink him in.

Straining to pull meaning from the man's chatter, Richard asked the sky for help. Flat and silver-gray, it lay powerfully over the woods, though neither God, who was surely up there, nor Jesus, offered more than silent breaths to sustain his body, his head, his ears, his brain, his soul.

Meanwhile, the two mortal voices rose and fell, talking about blame, accidents...*take this,* the taking-charge man said at one point, *your goddamn nose is running...*The other one, in a gravelly burst, blew his nose. *We oughtta get him outta here,* he uttered...and at once the wind picked up, rattling low branches, and in due time the voices faded to whispers and ghostly whispers to hums, drifting off like swamp fog curling, breaking up, disappearing back into the thickets.

Richard's eyes ached, the rest of him a mystery. Still, there was no real physical pain. No hurt in bones or muscle or organs.

After a while, a heavy loneliness set in. He drifted off and at some distant point felt the air stir. Opening his eyes, he watched the black wasp arrive. Felt it land, cross his chin, climb his furrowed cheek, and peer into his eyes. A curious little creature taking advantage of the situation to explore.

Eventually, the wasp moves down to a nostril, hesitates, and then makes its way inside like a spelunker exploring a cave. Richard feels a twitch and suddenly sneezes, lifts his large head a little, and sneezes again—this time sending the little demon scuttling into the air, only to disappear and return, landing in the cropped hair on Richard's head. He feels the little fellow making its way over his bristled scalp and, at once, something in his skull twitches and a finger on his right hand twitches as well, his pointer finger. With some concentration, he can curl it a little—nerves somewhere alert, connected. The toes in his right boot seem to want to come to life.

And Richard feels, without completely grasping it, a bit of hope, anticipation. He pictures the wound. The bullet, wherever it struck him, must have torn through a bundle of nerves and found its way to his spine. That's what happens, the spine suffers a blow and your body freezes up.

The wasp makes its way back to his nose, settles there. Richard imagines that, surely, before the shot was fired, his visitor was searching for crickets in the log he himself had commandeered as a resting place. Crickets eat larvae in rotting logs. Wasps eat crickets. Spiders suck life out of wasps. Lizards eat spiders. Foxes eat lizards. Men, they kill foxes and deer and each other for no natural reason. It all seems sinister, illogical that every creature God breathes life into becomes prey, but then, if God was logical, He wouldn't be God.

Straining his dry eyes, Richard glances down to get a blurred image of Mr. Wasp and, for the first time, thinks of something other than himself—Addie. She fills his mind. The scent of her breath and glowing skin. Her hands and fingers moving over the keys of the piano they had placed in a room they call "the parlor" and the one she once played at the Village Creek Club where they still go to dance on an occasional Saturday night. Their two daughters; Myra, a nurse way up in New York City, and the older one, Doreen, four years married and finally with child, something she has long promised.

Then, he glimpses the new lumber he arranged this morning on his workbench. He is a carpenter, a repairer, who turned himself into a cabinet and furniture maker. *Or had been.* Sitting quietly on the old log before the gun went off, he was contemplating the joints of a chair he is making for a woman to place in front of her antique desk, two hundred years old from West Virginia. She asked him to match the grain and ancient colors of the hand-hewn red oak. Something she knows he can do.

Without making a torment of it, Richard works at raising his head to look down on himself, twitching fingers on his right hand, toes on his right foot, managing it all without pain and a touch of satisfaction. It is tiring, this concentration, anticipation. He rests. The wasp remains on his nose as still and noble as one he might have carved from a piece of African ebony.

Richard begins to wonder how long a wasp can live and how much of his short life this stubborn warrior is devoting to keeping him company. Not an insignificant amount. Why? Was he sent by the seer Gabriel or was he just looking for a way to expand his education of the human world?

Managing a warm breath, Richard sees his daughter, Myra, wonders at the devotion she has toward helping people and how he could be even partially responsible for someone that good.

Time passes. Gradually, the soft, silver-gray patina begins to drain from the sky. Evening comes on. Doves, solitary and in groups of two and three, pass overhead on their way to the stock ponds and creeks and swamps that define the earth around here. Seeing them from a new perspective, their perfectly designed underwings, pointed heads, and sleek bodies play games with Richard's imagination so that through his weak glazed eyes, they seem to flock together and float. One of them, changing shape and glittering snow white, turns and dives toward him.

Yellow jackets. He recalls the yellow jackets. He must have been six or seven then, the first or second grade. Behind their house, down a slope, there was a creek that turned through a thicket of briars and bushes covered in honeysuckle vines. Crawling through there on hands and knees one summer day, he got into a nest of yellow jackets. They swarmed, stinging his hands, his arms, the top of his head. Scared crazy, he scrambled free and ran home, screaming, crying, nearly hysterical. His father, a big, ordinarily gentle man, came off the back porch and, hearing his story, grabbed his shoulders and shook him, shook him good. "Yellow jackets," he said. "Little biddy yellow jackets. If you're going to cry, save it for something worth crying about." His father dragged him into the kitchen, gave him soap and a box of baking soda, and told him to wash the tears and treat himself. It took all of the boy's forbearance to get through it—washing the prickly wounds, mixing the baking soda into a paste, dabbing it on to look like a clown's silly, white polka dots on his brown skin, the sting gone, at least in his mind, the minute he was done.

Late that afternoon, his father came home from the railroad yard where he worked with a sack of peaches, rock salt, and a block of ice. His mother put ice cream together. And under the porch roof, he and his brother took turns turning the crank that turned the paddles on the ice cream machine until they wouldn't turn any more and his father took over.

Now here he is on his back as vulnerable as a baby waiting to be lifted from a cradle, a Moses basket floating in reeds beside the Nile.

He prays but not so fervently as to be begging or making himself a nuisance. It is nearly dark, moonless, and sure to get darker fast. A few pale stars way up in the firmament. A chance that Venus is visible on a far horizon if only he can turn his head to see into the eastern sky. Mr. Wasp has left, heading back to his nest, his community, somewhere deep in the thickets where he has obligations to keep, no doubt.

Nightmarish thoughts: if a copperhead comes along, quietly slides up his pant leg, and curls around his balls to take a nap, he'll never know it. In fact, there could be one nosing around down there right now and no way to tell. What if the serpent gets bored and decides to bite? *What if the poison kills me?* he thinks. *I won't know that either.* In the moment of dying, you don't know it any more than you know the moment you fall asleep, not unless an angel appears to shake you awake or whisk you away. Which brings up a greater notion, one that has been milling around all this time in some bushy corner of his mind. Would Addie be better off if he gives it up here and now without a lot of fuss? Will his girls be better off?

Richard shakes his head and grunts. A chill washes through him and the words *hell no* fill his conscience as clear as the words of the minister when he gets wound up and disturbs the lilies in the stained-glass windows.

They will be coming. In his imagination, they are already calling around, organizing and will come in a parade of lights with long beams to light the woods, the creeks, the thickets. They will be yelling and calling his name—his wife, Doreen, his son-in-law, Myra's spirit, two brothers, a sister, friends, neighbors, and others. And they will find him and Addie will come and lift his head and start the healing. And after a struggle, he will be carving chairs again and they will push the door open to a fine morning and all that's new under the sun.

Acknowledgments

First, my sincere thanks to Kimberly Verhines, director of Stephen F. Austin State University Press, for publishing and overseeing the production of this book, and Karina Chacon for doing such a beautiful job designing it from cover to cover. Both are a joy to work with.

There are many others I must thank. My lifetime friend, C.W. Smith, much honored novelist, short story writer, and Emeritus Distinguished Professor of English at Southern Methodist University, who has been reading, encouraging, and helping improve my work for many years. Andrew Porter, the award-winning author and professor of English at Trinity University, for a wonderful seminar at the University of Iowa and encouraging my fiction from the time he read my first story. Polly Rosenwaike, author and fiction editor of *Michigan Quarterly Review*, who helped me edit and organize the collection. The agent, Nat Sobel, for early encouragement and being so generous with his time. The Emmy award-winning screenwriter, Marshall Riggan, for giving me my first paying job as a writer and teaching me to look for the story and drama even when writing commercial and promotional films. And in memory of my teacher at the Univeristy of Texas Graduate School of English, John Cherry Watson.

Among those who have helped keep me honest and sane, C. Patrick Payne, Tom Patterson, *and in memory*, Bill Dorough, and other good friends. And, of course, my family, Dean and Heidi Whitus, Amy and Venkat Krishnamurthy, and the heroic six, who give me hope for the future—Miranda, Nikhil, Simon, Ashwin, Vijay, and Vikram. And most of all my wife, Ann.

Born and raised in East Texas, Jerry Whitus received a bachelor's degree in international business and studied American literature and fiction writing in the graduate program at the University of Texas at Austin. His stories have been published in many leading literary journals, including the *Chicago Quarterly Review*, *Ploughshares*, the *Los Angeles Review*, and *MĀNOA*. Before turning to fiction, he spent years as a freelance writer specializing in film and video for education, industry, government, and entertainment. Productions he scripted have received many national awards, including three Silver Awards and the Award of Creative Excellence from the International Film and TV Festival of New York, two Silver Screen Awards from the US Industrial Film Festival of Chicago, the Gold Ring Award from the International Association of Business Communicators, two Best of Texas Awards from the Texas Public Relations Association, and first place at the USAID International Film Festival in Washington, DC. After receiving a master's degree in English as a Second Language, he has been a classroom teacher specializing in writing for international students, an administrator, and teacher-trainer in colleges and universities in the USA, Japan (where he also served in the U.S. Marine Corps), Singapore, Vietnam (on a USAID grant), and Colombia.

You may contact him at authorjerrywhitus@mail.com or visit the author online at jerrywhitus.wixsite.com/author.

Printed in the USA
CPSIA information can be obtained
at www.ICGtesting.com
JSHW022349091224
75127JS00001B/1